Between

LAURIE PETROU

Pedlar Press | Toronto

COPYRIGHT © Laurie Petrou 2006

ALL RIGHTS RESERVED. No part of this book may be reproduced or transmitted in any form or by any means whatsoever without written permission from the publisher, except by a reviewer, who may quote brief passages in a review.

PEDLAR PRESS
PO Box 26, Station P, Toronto Ontario M5S 2S6 Canada

ACKNOWLEDGEMENTS. The publisher gratefully acknowledges the financial support of the Canada Council for the Arts and the Ontario Arts Council for its publishing program.

LIBRARY AND ARCHIVES CANADA CATALOGUING IN PUBLICATION

Petrou, Laurie, 1976-
    Between / Laurie Petrou.

ISBN 1-897141-10-6

    I. Title.

PS8631.E865B48 2006   C813'.6   C2006-902729-3

First Edition

BOOK DESIGN
Zab Design & Typography | Winnipeg

TYPEFACES
(Body) Dolly
(Headings) Chalet

Printed in Canada

FOR MY FAMILY I love you

CONTENTS

Taxi	9
In the Home	13
Treasure	19
July Tile	26
With Love From	31
From Kentucky	36
Wedding Day	45
Fall	53
After Bingollo's	60
Paper Girl	66
Daycare	70
Butterfly Net	76

Taxi

HE WAS WATCHING the back of her neck with that old teen combo of innocence and lasciviousness. She was scratching her neck absently while flipping through the D's in the Rock section of Brian's Records. He was holding his navy blue duffle bag with one hand, with the index finger of his other hand he was holding a spot between two records. Madonna. McCartney. MaggieMaggie-MaggieMaggieMaggie. She licked her lips. What a lexicon of lust was written in his scrutiny of this mouth.

"Can I borrow that Dylan record off you?"

Nate shook himself as the mouth spoke to him. He turned back to the M's, blushing.

"I'll make you a tape."

The sun was burning through the dirty windows. He put the bag down, the handle of his tennis racket sticking out, a reminder of yet another loss to that black-haired beauty who now ran her hand over her freshly washed hair. She was in every way more than him, this girl of his Saturdays. She could volley and she could stroke and she could take hold. He was always losing his grasp. She flipped through the records rhythmically, turning one sneakered toe on its end. She turned to him.

"Do you want to go?"

"Okay."

They walked silently in the sun. Mid-day, mid-summer sun. The concrete was bone dry and there was little shade. Nate held a can of Coke to his cheek, he fingered the change in his pocket. Maggie turned her head and hailed a cab. The car slowed to a halt. They climbed onto the hell-hot leather seats and burned their fingers on the seatbelts. Nate felt himself melting: down, down, through the leather, dripping through the seat stuffing, through the car parts he knew nothing about, onto the seared asphalt, flattened by the tires of this car that held damp Maggie and her magnificent mouth. She gave directions. Nate looked out the window, grimy and filmy, at the blur of low office buildings and sidewalks. He thought of train trips he'd taken with his mother: north or west, further away. He always sat facing the back of the train, feeling like the countryside was rushing out of his ears. On the way home, he'd switch seats so he could imagine the fields hitting him hard in the chest. His hometown was not a landscape. It was a parking lot. Plazas. Not small town, small school, small creeks, small stores. Not downtown bustle-on-Bloor either. It was concrete, but not skyscraper. It was anonymity—not for size, but for lack of interest. Nate turned to Maggie. She worked at the drugstore: *Open to Midnight*. Sometimes she stole eyeliner. Read the magazines off the shelves when there was nothing to do.

"My Dedo—my grandfather—" he blinked, "he used to have a restaurant around here."

Her mouth turned up into a sip of a smile. He wanted to tell her a story. But which one, and how many? He wanted to tell stories all day, break the floodgates, talk and blurt and point and confess. She had the kind of face you could tell stories to. If you gasped, she'd gasp right along with you, her mouth opening into a small O, parroting enthusiasm. But *his* stories? At home, in the dense dark, he listened to a Gentle Waves song on the wrong speed and thought he could feel the beauty of it under his nails and blushing on his knees. This was his story. He frowned.

"What was it called?"

"What?"

"The restaurant."

Nate bit his thumbnail. "Taxi. He called it Taxi, because when he first came here he drove a taxi, and … and so he called it Taxi," he finished lamely. She looked at him.

It wasn't in slow motion, like those sorts of things should be. Suddenly the car was spinning across two lanes and then screaming its metal—grey on grey—across the guardrail. It lurched to a stop. Maggie was unfastening her seatbelt. The taxi driver was thumping feebly at his chest, and Marvin Gaye and Tammy Terrell were belting out "Ain't Nothin' Like the Real Thing." Nate sat, a lump, un-heroic, proving there are indeed two kinds of people in this world, not even *moving*. He sat and watched.

Maggie got out of the car. The door banged on the guardrail. She went to the driver's door and opened it. The driver's head was thrown back and he was still. His tongue lolled. Maggie undid his seatbelt. She reached down in between his large legs and adjusted his seat so it moved backwards and then horizontal. His large profile rushed downward, beside and below Nate. Maggie lifted two soft fingers against stubbled jowls. She tipped back the driver's face, opened his mouth. Wet hair clung to his forehead, some rogue curls hung down. She reached into the mouth, circling inside it with her fingers as though she'd been there a thousand times. She hovered over him, her knees on either side of one of his bulky thighs. She pinched his nostrils and licked her lips. Her chest filled as her mouth took in the rotten air of the cab, and she pressed it against the driver's mouth. Took a breath and passed it to him, her hair grazing his wide face. Two more times. His chest heaved. Now he was coughing and sputtering and crying. Maggie turned his head sideways and rubbed his back. There there. She pushed a curl over his ear. There there. A string of saliva crossed the distance from his face to his shoulder. He raised his eyes. Clear and blue and full.

"Will you move your ass? God, no wonder you've never won a tennis match."

They were ambling along the shoulder now. Crisis averted. Maggie had worked the radio to call for help. Nate knew why he'd never won a tennis match. Maggie took long strides slightly ahead of him, running her hand along the guardrail. She hadn't looked at him directly since before it happened. Her voice sounded different. He tried to catch up. The arm of his racket banged into his shin and he stumbled. She laughed quietly. A car drove past, and then another.

"Maggie." He'd never said her name before. She turned her head to the side, waiting.

In the Home

WHAT CAN I REMEMBER from when I was sixteen, seventeen? Fragments, snapshots, smells. Mostly smells. I don't remember more than the average person, and I'm older than the average person. But I keep repeating stories. People keep asking. I retell so many things from those years that my memories have crystallized into some kind of sour slideshow even I know enough to question the staginess of. My brother was buried under a bombed-out building and I dug him out with my bare hands; my life was saved by a faulty parachute; the war came to a halt momentarily in a brothel. The headlines of my life, touted by my children and grandchildren. *Ask your grandfather, he was in the war.* I'd correct the mistakes if I could remember the truth as something stretching beyond smells and moments. What do you remember from that age? Do all the years in between matter as much? The pity is that these memories, these stories, which may not even be mine for all the connection I feel, are my last ticket to credibility. They are all I can be trusted with; the only time I'm not a threat to conversation. They are mine, as much as they don't feel like it. A dusty burden. I can't be trusted to drive a car, but I'm expected to remember with clean and exact recall something that happened sixty years ago. Back then I had tried to forget it, not knowing that age would take care of that, or that it would become a staple of respectable conversation.

I also remember other things, small things from the

years before and after. Things no one cares about or wants to hear. I remember working as a junior bartender at the social club. Bringing drinks to the women. Corn dogs and ale and cigarettes. I remember last week, if just some of it. I know that Wednesdays are kind days even though I don't work anymore. Thursdays are the best. Almost the weekend but no calendar plans, no hangover, no looming Sunday. Thursday evenings still stretch out before me with promise. What'll I do? What'll I do with my Thursday?

My son comes to visit. I'm not in a home yet, but staying with a friend, Jim. He's older than I am, so how this is supposed to be easier for me I don't know. He takes up space, gets me nervous. When he rattles up those stairs in his too-long corduroys I just know he's going to trip one of these times and I'll end my days giving mouth-to-mouth to that sour old windbag. I always refused to go into a home, but I didn't think they'd actually listen to me when it came down to it. I should have asked while the asking was good, gotten a condo or something, but now I'm here like I'm acting out a Lemmon and Matthau movie. When my son comes I can see him from the window. I love watching him park so carefully, like he's docking a ship, and he brushes his hand over his forehead before he jogs across the street. Sometimes he brings my granddaughter. She's nine. Last time she was here Jim tried to teach her that game where you spread your fingers on the table and stab in between them with a knife.

It's Thursday now. I know this because Jim has gone to the club early to get a good seat for the corned beef and cabbage. My son is coming. I straighten up the house. Dust the top of the television and shake out the curtains. I turn on the radio, loud, so I can hear it upstairs while cleaning the bathroom. I didn't hear my son come in and was sorry that I missed him pull up. When your kids are young, you get to spy on them all the time. When they're grown you can't do it anymore. They say What? What? all the time. Nothing! Nothing. I didn't want the house to smell like old people, so I sprayed Fantastic all over the bathroom and of course now all my son hears is me coughing.

"Dad? Dad! Are you okay?" He comes running up the stairs.

"Jesus! Dad, you don't have to use so much of this stuff." As he helps me down the stairs, he tells me to watch my pants.

We eat together. The fridge hums. I make sandwiches. I worry about whether the food is fresh enough. I watch him eating his sandwich.

"How is work?"

"Fine. It's fine. I get bored sometimes, but they've laid some people off, so I guess I should be thankful I have a job." He looks out the window, a few minutes go by.

"Were you ever bored? Did you ever want to leave your job? I mean, you were there for so many years."

"Sure. Sometimes I fantasized about walking out," I say. Sometimes, is the truth, I fantasized about beating up my manager and driving as far south as I could. "But, you know, I guess I grew out of that." That's a lie. Now I fantasize about beating up the kid at the LCBO if he takes too long. Or that snippy little cook at the club. Sometimes I give Jim a shove, too, but he is a pretty big guy even though he's older than me.

"Yeah," says my son. He helps me clear the dishes. After that, we go out to the garden and look at the vegetables. He pulls out the weeds I haven't gotten to yet. I fill a bucket with tomatoes for him. It's quite hot today and when I straighten up I can feel my back sweating through my shirt. I have to take a leak, but know that my son wouldn't approve of that sort of thing. Actually, urine is very good for a garden. I go back inside, banging the screen door behind me.

Upstairs, out the bathroom window, I can hear my son talking to the neighbour. I can't hear what he's saying, but I'm not trying. He's probably checking up on me. Making sure I'm not climbing trees or the roof or anything. Maybe not. Maybe he's asking my neighbour if he ever gets bored at his job.

When I come back downstairs, my son is looking at a picture of me next to my tank, in Italy. It's in a small frame in a niche in the hall. There's a light over it and everything. The niche is a very good spot for a picture, but this one is a little small and pale—not up to the job. He looks at me and smiles and I can tell he's searching my face for the boy in the picture. I wonder if this makes him doubt me now that he is twice as old as I was when I experienced the things I tell him about.

He knows what it's like to be seventeen. He looks like he feels sorry for me, though. I figure that's because he has a child now. All children are your own after you've had a child, even your parents in old pictures. I take the picture out of his hands and give him a pat on the shoulder.

It's fall. The trees are turning and this old street is warm and bright, the leaves starting to cover the sidewalk. I leave my windows open for one last taste of fresh air before they are locked for the winter. I start to wear more layers. I cover my rose bushes with burlap, which snaps in the wind, threatening to pick up and whirl away. Holding it down, I tie tight knots around the bases. Proper knots. People don't know how to make proper knots anymore. As though there's no use for knots in a world of computers and snow blowers.

This morning when I wake, there is frost. It's dark in my room and the floor is cool under my bare feet. I wrap my arms around myself and turn on lights as I make my way through the house. When my wife was alive we would make fires on days like this. Close the doors and turn inward, turn toward each other, watching the news, watching the shows. Now I don't make fires. It's so quiet here, but I feel happy. Today I'm going to go to the club and maybe play a couple of hands of cards. Flirt a little with Rose, maybe. Have fish and chips.

The club is hopping, as much as old people can cause a room to hop. It's one of those days, I can tell. At the beginning of spring and at the end of fall, days are sunny and crisp and have a Last Chance feel about them. On days like this everyone makes it over to the club.

The building is old and the stores on either side have changed ownership many times over the years. The club itself has been owned by a father and son for a number of years: Wiseman and Son. Pete Wiseman is short and leathery and large of hands and heart. His son is wiry and slick. None of us like him much, namely because he put a stop to our long-standing tabs when he started helping out his dad. Probably for the better: We would've run Pete into the ground under a heap of beer and smoked meat.

I have spent a few hours at the club. I lost ten dollars to that rat Connelly with his lousy squeaky laugh, filled myself with chips and fish and ginger ale and the one beer I let myself have, nursing it over the afternoon. Rose never asks if I want another. I push my chair out and brush crumbs from my lap, wave to Jim and point to my watch. I don't know why I do that. I never like Jim staying out later than me.

I've gotten about a block when I hear heels clicking after me. Rose, her red hair glimmering in the setting sun, apron strings waving out behind her, is running after me, carrying my coat.

"You forgot this again," she says. "And you forgot to pay, too, but Jim says he'll pick it up." I feel my neck reddening. Lately I've been forgetting things at the club. Last week it was my cards and wallet. Rose looks so pretty. I feel like an old dog. I thank her and she smiles, rubbing her arms. She turns and heads back, her heels clicking against the sidewalk. It reminds me of something, but I can't remember what. I kick at a pile of leaves.

When I open the door to my house, I feel unsettled. It smells wrong or something. I'm hot, and I shed my jacket right where I am, letting it fall to the floor. My eyes are tired. It's just a change in climate, I tell myself. My mouth is dry and I'm dizzy. I put my hands on my bent legs and try to slow down my breathing. I lift my head and walk down the hallway to the kitchen. But this is not my house. I've walked into someone else's goddamned house. Fool.

How can I be doing this? I'm like a child, a goddamned child. I pick up a spoon and hold it up to my face. What a joke. My arm falls to my side. The kitchen is nice. It seems brighter than mine, and it is: They've a bigger window out to the yard. They should wrap those young cedars out there.

It's like seeing another version of my life. What if I'd knocked down a wall? What if we'd wallpapered? What if I'd married a woman who loved miniature figurines like these? I hold the china figure up close and look into the painted face. Her eyes, little black lines, are upturned in a happy grimace. Suddenly someone screams, a frankly quite homely teenaged girl with braces, holding a phone.

"There's a fucking old pervert in my house! Get OUT! What the fuck are you doing here? What the fuck is he doing here? Call the police! I'm calling the police. GET OUT OF HERE!"

I'm with my son again. My other children are here also and they are having a meeting of sorts. They're talking like I'm not here. I start whistling.

"Dad. Stop that." *Stop that*. I mimic with my lips. It was only a mistake, for godsakes. Wait until Jim finds out. I hate this. Stupid. I kick the table leg.

"Dad. Stop."

In the end, they agree to tell me simply: Be more careful. I know that my days are numbered.

I am careful. I wash the counters all the time. I use vinegar instead of ammonia. I pay attention. It's looming, I know, but if I'm just more careful, I can keep things as they are just a little longer. I can see the 'retirement' home on my way to the club. *Come On!*, I want to say, *I'll break you all out of there! Let's go stir it up!* But then I remember: *Be more careful*.

Treasure

EVERYONE ON OUR STREET HAD TWO BOYS. They are my boys: The boys I grew up with. I dropped into their world like a dirty pink bomb. But look: See how that bomb goes on unreleased. Rolling through an empty street like a threat.

There they are, the Fenway Road boys. It is the summer solstice, the longest day of the year, the first day of summer, Thursday. My parents have one boy already, and into the car goes my pregnant mum with the promise of perhaps another boy on the street of boy-oh-boy-oh-boys.

Take it from the bottom, boys! The houses line up like soldiers, garage doors like tucked-in shirts and roofs like combed hair.

Number 9, Tudor-style, manicured lawn. The Whites: Steven and Stuart. When I am four, I will tell my parents that when I get married my husband and I will live in the crawlspace under the stairs. I think that my husband will be Stuart White.

Number 13, backing onto the high school track where many maker-outers and first-time smokers will try their luck. Here live The Richardsons: Calvin and Andy. Mrs. Richardson will babysit and teach me songs about the vowels: Aye lyek tye ayet ayet ayepples ayend bye-nye-nyes.

Number 14, a wide lawn and a barking Dalmatian. The Diamonds: Leo and Max. At age five, Max will routinely tell us our parents' car is a piece of shit. Leo will grow up to be a model, a strutting suburbanite. Those Diamond boys: Long eyelashes and fast legs.

Number 16, the house is our double on the inside—a split bungalow, which feels the same but then strikes unfamiliar in its smells and styles. The Smarts: Matt and Nick. Such nice boys. They will take over the family business. As a child, Matt will make a yo-yo out of lifesavers and string for a neighbourhood magic show. He will somehow swallow the yo-yo, causing awe in children and alarm in parents. After much coughing and crying, the wet and tangled string will resurface without the yo-yo. We will applaud.

Number 18: Our house. The car door slams, my mum on the passenger side. Sandra Dee hair and a pink shift dress. Dad turns the key, rolls the car into the street. It stops for just a moment before changing gears. Look at the wooden sign, swinging on hinges, squeaking 18, 18. Look at the house, the young maple tree, the shyly growing perennials. Look at Grandma in the doorway, holding my brother who holds the doll he's taken to dragging around by the foot. Wave goodbye now, blow kisses.

And then I'm home, pink on a street of blue. Do I dust myself off, spit in your eye, whistle with two fingers like the big boys? I consider this, and choose instead to sit poolside. Yessir, she's got a thumb-sucker's eye for comfort, that girl. All boom and no bust. I'm a boy-watcher, a boy-watcher.

My brother was in his room with a torn and rumpled paperback. I was kicking my legs under the table and watching my mother for a gap when she wouldn't assign a chore, or ask a pointed question about the upcoming science fair or the state of the pile of clothes on my bed. She turned toward the sink and reminded my father that she was *one hundred percent sure* of whatever he couldn't remember. I ducked out, sleuth-like. I backed along the hallway and out the screen door, which stuck open unless you pushed it. I squinted and blew the smoke off my gun finger.

I hopped off the two-step porch and looked along the street. A few houses down, little Max Diamond, his older brother Leo and Andy Richardson were fixing a bike chain. Max's tuneless, high-pitched singing of "Wasn't that a Party" belied the boozy lyrics. *Coulda been the two, four, six-pack, I dunno, but look at the mess I'm in! My head is like a football! I think I'm gonna diiiiie.* I made an X on a mosquito bite on my ankle and then scuffed my shoes all the way over. *Tell me: Me, oh, me, oh, my. Wasn't that a Party.*

"What are you doing?"

"What does it look like?"

Leo leaned over the bike pedal, limp hair in his eyes. I kicked him in the bum. He reached back and swiped at me, I grabbed the handlebar and jumped backward, ringing the bike bell twice to show off.

"Wanna go with us to the park, Ellie? We're gonna make a ramp and bike off of it!"

"Shut up, Max!" Leo looked at me. "No, we're not. And you can't come."

"Too bad, I'm coming."

Andy looked over and smiled apologetically, which made me feel better. He is the nice one, I thought, although earlier I'd drawn a picture of him with a dartboard around it in my journal. I ran back and got my bike out of the garage. I had to pedal like crazy to catch up with them, then sped ahead and stuck my legs out straight, coasting. Andy whistled.

At the park, they erected a ramp using a large piece of plywood that Andy had carried on the front of his handlebars. I wasn't all that interested—not big on scraped knees or bloody lips. I kicked at the sand. Surveyed the grass for dog crap. I made a couple of lopsided somersaults. I wandered around, slapping trees with my palms. *Slap slapslap slap.*

I could hear the creek in the distance. It lay at the bottom of the hill that we tobogganed down in the winter. It always scared me, that creek and its foreboding proximity to the hill. Steven White's friend had gone all the way down and into it, busting his wrist. Screaming like a maniac at the bottom, and we had to run home, sweating in our snow pants, to get our parents. We came back in the car, he was sitting at the side of the creek, soaking wet and whimpering.

A mid-sized stone stuck out of the earth, sort of like a gravestone. Something was written on it in marker, and I knelt down, holding my breath.

I could hear the boys, dully in the background. Max was crying.

"Stop crying, come on. My mom is going to kill me."

"It's okay, Maxxy, it'll just be a bump. Hey! Let's run our dinky cars off the ramp and see whose goes the farthest!"

I heard them scrambling up. Max was snivelling. I leaned in on the stone. *Stay Away Do Not Touch*. My heart raced. My throat was thick with urgency. The dirt came away in fistfuls. *Yo Ho Ho! The Curse of the Fenway Road Treasure!* About a foot down, pretty freshly buried, was a damp shoebox. I got a chill, thinking it might be a dead hamster like the one in the shoebox in front of our basketball net at home. I clawed at the dirt surrounding the box.

"What are you doing? What is that?"

It was Leo. Andy and Max had followed him.

"I dunno." I put my hand on the lid.

Time Capsil Do Not Open till 2050, the top of the box read in the same scrawl. Leo laughed.

"That is so stupid!"

I laughed too, thinking it ingenious.

I put the lid aside. We all leaned into one another, our skin goosebumpy, our breath hot and close. Andy and I bumped heads, which made my scalp tingle. Inside the box: A locket shaped like a big oval, with a chain; a Transformer; a picture of four people standing in a grassy field, a mom, a dad, a boy and a girl, and in the background—tiny, tiny—another girl, chasing a small brown and white dog that had turned around to look at her, its tongue lolling; a bag of Fool's Gold candy; a folded up page of *The Toronto Star* that didn't have much in it but the headline *Charles and Diana to Visit*—it was from two weeks ago.

Max picked up the locket, rolling it in his fingers. The sun caught the engraved detail of two overlapping hearts.

"Just like real treasure," he murmured.

"Yeah," said Leo, "and I'm takin' this Transformer!"

He grabbed it and Andy blurted out, "No, don't!" I said he was right, we shouldn't, and karate chopped Leo's wrist for good measure. We bickered about it for a while until Andy pushed Leo and threatened to break the Transformer. There was some more squabbling, and some general complaints about what had been left in the capsule in the first place. And then we sort of lost interest, and Leo said he didn't want someone else's crummy old used toy anyway, and we jointly decided to put something in the box so that whoever put it there would know we had found it. We agreed on a note because no one wanted to leave anything of their own in the box, but we were undecided on the message.

"It should say, Dig the hole deeper next time, retard."

"No, it should say, I'm an alien and I've come to take over your planet. Take me to —— no, um, now I can be one of you, 'cause I have all this stuff."

"It should say, Busted, and I'll draw a skull on it."

"It should say, I am a Transformer trapped in a box. And I learned to write."

Finally we agreed on, Greetings from the Fenway Pirates. Guard your treasure better. Lucky for you we just stole some other booty.

We closed the box and covered it with earth as the sky started to fall. Clouds had gathered, and the rain made our bikes cool and slick as we rode out of the park. It was teeming by the time I jumped the curb and hit our street. I sped ahead of everyone else until I was riding alone in a concrete frontier. I was an explorer, discovering our street and all the empty houses and could choose which house I wanted for my own. When I heard the boys' voices gaining on me, I growled. I felt irritated in a defensive way—like when I get caught in a big lie. Rain pelted my scalp like an icy comb.

I brooded all evening. It burdened me like an itch, and I picked at a scab on my knee until my mum threatened to tie my fingers. What I wanted, in that hot and possessive, restricting way, was the picture in the box. I wanted the girl chasing the dog. I hated the thought of the wet shoebox in the shallow earth, imagined worms and worse crawling into the moistened cardboard, the colours of the picture blanching into rain. I watched the rain-streaked windows as night came.

I had never skipped school but I knew it was done. I had seen other kids—older kids—walking past the windows, strutting under jealous eyes, smoking and spitting and waving.

My bike was still a little wet from the night before, and I wheeled it into the morning sun. I would have no problem showing up late for school. I was a good kid, suspicions of hooky didn't stretch to the likes of me, a daydreamer content to scribble in the margins. I sort of wished I was more troublesome, a child at risk of running off to join the circus. But today I was proud and slick and smooth—and about to add *bad* to my list.

The air was still. At school, students would be pulling their chairs under them as teachers closed doors with a click and a 'Now.'

The grass at the park was wet. I leaned my bike against the swings, strange and lonely, hanging limp on their chains. Finding the spot was easy. We had done a pretty lousy job of burying the box. There was a large mound instead of even earth, and the marker looked clumsily replaced. I held out my arms, trying to gain my balance in the muddy ground. I hadn't accounted for this, and had no choice but to kneel in the mud, feeling my knees go instantly wet through my cotton pants. This would cause me trouble later with my mother. I sunk my fingers into the wet earth.

I felt sad, sort of, felt like lying back and giving myself over to the cool and damp and slimy ground. I was embarrassed about wanting the picture. I was embarrassed of everything anyway, which made me more embarrassed, and embarrassment toppled onto itself like a reeking pile. I was hot and itchy and sweaty and aware of myself. I had spent years following the boys and keeping up, outdoing, outsmarting, holding my breath longer. But now I suddenly knew better than to lie in the mud. My cowboy confidence was slipping, and I wasn't sure if I wanted it back, or some soft and pretty alternative that itself seemed like an impossible transformation.

The toy alone was bright and glistening, and I thought of my brother's toys at the edge of our bathtub, luminous plastic. The newspaper was soggy and ruined. The candy had vanished. The picture was turned on its back. It almost fell apart in my fingers. The girl and the dog had a patch of mud smeared over them. I tried to wipe it away, and the image went with it, right off the photo paper. I put the smallest patch of what was left in my breast pocket, looked at my mud-streaked fingers and nails and wiped my nose with the sleeve of my jacket.

Years before, my father gave me an oversized purse—a lady purse. It was white turtle-shell with a glittery clasp. I filled it with my Hallowe'en candy and stashed it in the basement. That summer, the summer we had a heat wave and an invasion of ants, I dressed up like Sleeping Beauty and wanted the purse for effect. I found it behind an old car seat. All the candy had melted and it was full of dead ants. They were stuck, in and out of the chocolate muck, like victims of a miniature bomb.

Keep your eye on the bomb, now, pretty and pink, unreleased.

July Tile

RON'S HOUSE IS LIKE OURS, a proud post-war semidetached. His is half red and half grey, his side being the red half. I've been there so many times, it's mine too, meaning it is right up there with the things that make me feel comfortable, relaxed. This is our street and these are our houses and we've gone back and forth between them for so long that I've stopped noticing anything in between.

I remember one time, the owner of the hardware store on the block that separates our houses had pleaded with me to repaint Ron's garage after Ron had painted it orange. Like he didn't care that it wasn't actually my house. The neighbours who have the grey half of Ron's place paved their garden and put a fountain of Jesus in the middle of four concrete slabs. Water pumps out of his palms all day long. The fountain has been dying for our sins for at least fifteen years.

The day was a stunner and my toolbox banged against my leg, pinching hairs, which were moist with sweat. I winced in the sun. I tried to suck my stomach in. I held it for a few seconds and then exhaled, giving it an apologetic pat as I turned into the walkway. A small pile of stringy weeds lay in a heap next to the open door.

Ron was in the kitchen. He came into the hall and wiped his brow with an oven-mitted hand.

"Come in and taste this."

I looked up the steep stairs before following him into the kitchen. The carpet on the stairs was wearing thin and I knew my feet shared this responsibility. I thought of a New Year's party about ten years ago. Aggie had tied a cluster of noisemakers and hung them at the top of the stairs like mistletoe. Coming out of the bathroom, teetering like a creaky old toy, I'd stood on my toes to blow into one of them, and lost my balance just as my lips touched the mouthpiece. I whirled around on the spot and grabbed a picture on the wall, holding it with both hands to regain my balance. It was a photo of Ron's grandfather. He stared back at me, unsmiling in uniform, his gun over his shoulder. I leaned forward and kissed him on the mouth, then got embarrassed and stood back and saluted him, smacking my head again on the noisemaker mistletoe. Julie applauded me from the bottom of the stairs.

I climbed the stairs now, heaving myself up with the help of the banister, the heat like its own champagne. I opened the bathroom door and met after-shower fog. I put down my toolbox with a clang. It was a relief to let it go. The stacked black and white tiles that Ron and Aggie had chosen and that I'd piled against the far wall last time I was there were covered with dust and large drops of water. A towel lay in a wet lump in the corner, and the mirror was fogged. I pointed a finger at it but then could think of nothing to write or draw. Nothing to say. *Wash Me. Bloody Mary.* A face. A line. A dick. Two boobs and a triangle. I settled down among the tools and other things I'd brought and began wiping down the floor with the towel. Ron called up from the kitchen.

"How's Julie?" and then "Shit!" as he likely burned himself. I pictured him with his finger in his mouth, waiting for my response.

"Fine. Fine thanks."

I looked at the bathroom floor and didn't know where to begin or to feel like beginning. I lifted one tile and felt its weight and replaced it on the stack. An ant scurried out from behind the toilet carrying a fly's wing on its back.

I heard Aggie come out of the downstairs bedroom. She and Ron exchanged a kiss, a laugh. She came upstairs, into the doorway, and stood with wet hair, hands on hips, and I knew she was happy to see me.

"Sir Gregory, darling." She clasped her hands to her chest. "Are we going to have the floor I've always dreamed of?" She leaned into the doorframe. "How's our Julie?"

"Excellent. Pass me that. Excellent."

"Yeah?"

I smiled. "She's begging me to dance with her. Can you blame her?"

She rolled her eyes. "Do you want something to drink?" I said yes, please, that would be lovely, and felt like a formal guest.

"My pleasure," she winked.

I pulled my finger through the dust on a black tile, and the glaze shone. The inexorable heat of the day was close and palpable and made the room smaller. I inhaled, filling my lungs with air that made me feel constricted, the gentle suffocation of a hot bathroom. What was the matter with me? There were so many ways things could go wrong that it struck me as strange that more people weren't bed-bound with indecision. I pushed my shoes and socks off in a slight panic.

For Julie's birthday this year I gave her a cane. Julie broke her legs. Both of them, in different places. She is heavier now, and before it happened sometimes her legs hurt her and she walked with a slight limp even though we aren't yet at that age. We were out for dinner when it happened. It was a special occasion and I was wearing a V-neck sweater that made me itch. The restaurant was new to us and I was a little nervous; I guess we hadn't been out on a date in a long time. She looked spectacular. Had her hair done and everything. She looped her arm through mine and I felt like I might lift off the ground.

It was a Japanese restaurant, which our daughter had recommended. There were a lot of young people there and I felt overdressed and over-something, but good, good. The girls working there were so nice and I felt big and sweaty and like I might fall into the glass counter with all the raw fish. Julie gave my arm a squeeze. When we were sitting down she told me that the hot cloth wasn't for my face, but no one was looking so go ahead.

After dinner we headed over to Boxgrove Park and climbed

the stairs up to the war statue there. We didn't get to the top, there are so many steps, but still we could see the park from above and see people out on dates, or coming home late from work. I kissed Julie on the top of her head. We sat on the steps and shared a cigarette, and the smoke curled up around us. I stretched back onto the stair above me and spread my arms. The steps were cold and damp, but it was staying lighter later—winter was almost done—and the steps still had some day warmth to them. A dog chased a flock of birds in the park below; birds flew up through the trees with a rustle and then settled down again.

What happened was she fell when we were getting up. The way she lay at the bottom, the ambulance guys thought maybe she'd hurt her neck or something. They asked her her name and address. I told them and they said, no sir, we need to hear your wife say it. But her head wasn't hurt, it was her straw legs. I told her to watch the birds that were flying over as they lifted her soft body onto the stretcher. She winced and closed her eyes instead.

I told them to put her in the guest room because it was cooler. I was sweating like crazy and grunted as I leaned over the bed and pushed up the window. They laid her across the bed on top of clothes that needed ironing. The last winter wind drew in the curtain. The arm of a blue plaid dress pushed out under her waist and hung down the side of the bed. Her legs were covered in two white casts, lumpy in parts. I got her some water, and a cloth for her forehead, and after she fell asleep I got a marker and wrote, *This one is my favourite* on her left leg, and *I like it in here* on her right. I wrote it so she could read it from where she was if she were standing up.

I guess that was the wrong choice, that hand-carved olive wood cane with the effing duck head on top, which is what she said when she swiped it at me, wielding the duck like it was carved just for her hand, the last thing she wanted.

Years ago, before Jesus and tiles and broken legs, I was a sinewy wisp, a whisper, light on my feet, with a stiff hat and a smart walk. Julie was the feather. She was hair in the gust and if you didn't hold her back she'd fly out the third floor window.

We took dance lessons at Miss Tanahill's. There were big

windows that showed all the streetcars and traffic jams below. We were on the third floor with the Tango and the Waltz. Even an accident looks beautiful to a tango. Especially that. One day that did happen, and the class gathered at the window. Doors slammed and two drivers swore and waved and chased each other around a Volkswagen Rabbit.

Miss Tanahill was lithe and wrapped in muscle. She favoured scarves and flowing skirts. Her hair danced around her head like one of her crazy scarves. Julie and I saw her at the bank once and under her trench coat she wore a bright blue asymmetrical skirt. We imagined her sipping Chartreuse and listening to Marlene Dietrich in a darkly-painted apartment. She rode her bike everywhere, skirts and scarves billowing out behind her, apples in the basket. She looked like she could ride the wind in an upward squall. She'd had the dance studio for fifteen years.

Before we got big, before we got old and stiff, we were good dancers. Maybe we were just learning, but we had it down sometimes.

Aggie had brought me lemonade and toast and jam. Sort of an odd combination, the jam making the lemonade so bitter, but it was okay, it was a comfort. Some people always like toast and jam even when they get older and it's the middle of a summer day and there are fresh stuffed peppers available. I was halfway across the bathroom on my knees, finishing the floor. Black white black white black. White black white black white. The glass of lemonade now clinked over the tiles as I moved it with me. I was hurrying because I was thinking of shoes. There were two pairs that I knew Julie would like: A red pair with a flower cut out of leather and a black pair with a pale blue stripe over the toe. I hadn't chosen yet. If I hurried I could make it to the store on my way home.

With Love From

I TURN THE TAP WITH MY TOES and hold my feet under cold water until I can't bear it and then plunge them back into the bath. I'm not the first handsome young man to stay in the tub too long, using up all the water, catching my death of cold, hogging the bathroom. No Irish Rose standing outside my door, I am young only by old-man standards, handsome only by my own. I don't know any other men who take baths, except my father, who, contrary to the whole premise of a bath, will go in only after my mother is finished with the water. Designed for petite women and children, baths are not for men. Men in baths are always bent, the awkwardness of our bodies betrayed by damp and chilled hair slicked against pale skin, caved-in chests. This is why, I think, as I sink lower and lower and finally rest my earlobes on the water's surface, that men are never photographed in the tub. A woman I used to date, a quiet, charming person with very little sense of privacy, once swaggered in while I was taking a bath and took my picture. The idea of my petrified face (among other things), weird self-conscious posture and withered and pickled skin making their way if not across the internet, then at least across a table of howling girlfriends (one of whom always ferociously maintained I had a cheating nature) makes me anxious. I hold my breath and sink below the surface.

Today I will tell my father that I have sold his business. He is on his way, and I know that he has ironed his shirt, has shaved in the shower and then shaved again the missed spots close against the mirror. He has talked to my mom from the bathroom, and gone downstairs for his tea. He has cash in his wallet and letters to mail. He took the grocery list with him. I sold his business. My dad owned a paper shop. Stationery, envelopes, stamps, all things required in the communication of love, sympathy, apology and friendship. It is a well-liked store with a kind of cult status, known as a place that cares about the importance of design, the beauty of a carefully tied, leather-bound journal, the pleasure of an imprinting wax seal. It is called *With Love From*. Let that sink in. What kind of son would sell his father's store called *With Love From*? I am out of the tub now, mopping my face and hair with a towel, slapping my cheeks twice even though I don't wear aftershave. I whistle hollowly as I leave the room.

I'd made sure that the new owners would keep the name, and also made sure, perhaps against better business judgment, that I sold it to people who had not only really liked the shop, but whom I had seen as regular customers over the years. Nothing will change. They are even going to keep the staff, including, as it does, a terribly grumpy man and a woman with an awful habit of singing to herself. Not that that's a reason to let someone go, but really, a terrible voice.

I started working at *With Love From* when I was seventeen. For a seventeen-year-old, the pleasure which thirty-five-year-olds find in lovely and expensive raised embossed paper is irrelevant and annoying. Also high on my list of annoying things were the way my hair grew, my entire family and all the things that made me sad as well as annoyed. As I grew, I began, as we all do, to appreciate things more, to wise up. I tried to become interesting, interested, engaged. I think most people do this. I also think that as we wise up we start to find seventeen-year-olds annoying, and so we keep on at that age-old relationship where each age is pretty much disgusted by the one that it has just left behind.

I've written a lot of letters on paper from the shop. I have chosen the most beautiful black-as-spades pens and carved out the truth on soft, patterned paper. My loves, my ideas, my self, spilling like an accident. Dear Angie, I don't know what happened, but I am so sorry. I'm not sure exactly what I did, but I love you so much and I really want to make this work. I wish you were here right now and not at school. I wish I could drive up and see you right now. I know we can fix this. Dear Nat, You would love Calgary. The people are hilarious. I've actually seen a number of what seem to be real gall darn cowboys! Dear Olive, It was so nice meeting you. I feel like I could have talked to you all night, into the week, for the rest of the month and never run out of things to say. Dear Lynn, Thank you so much for your helpful suggestions. Your advice and generosity are much appreciated. Dear Dad, I sold the business. I know it's not what you wanted or expected, but I just think we (me and the business) will be better for it. I wish this were a real letter because I'm really dreading having to tell you this.

He gave me the option. He was done with the business, he said, and instead of leaving it to me in his will he wanted to turn it over to me now and said that if an offer ever came, or an opportunity knocked, I could sell the business and start out, like on the wild frontier. He never wanted me to feel stuck, and, he claimed, now that he'd unstuck himself from it, it was very plausible that the shop's time with us had ended. Naturally I absolutely refused this generous burden knowing that I can usually be counted on to do the wrong thing. My brother never showed any interest in the business, but neither, it can be said, did I. Pete doesn't feel slighted, he probably knows something I don't. Also he's loaded. My brother is an investment banker with wide and varied interests, many languages under his belt and the comfort of being a wonderful guy. He slapped me on the shoulder and told me to let him know if I needed to invest the earnings. I wouldn't consider myself a wonderful guy necessarily. I'm a good son, though, but now what do I do, I thought. I am a graduate student who inherited a paper shop from my father who is very much alive.

When people—kind and interested, non-invasive, inquisitive—ask me what I am writing my dissertation on, I often tell them that they don't want to know, which is not only probably true but also driven by a protective desire not to expose the ongoing, unending, twenty-storey house of cards that is my dissertation. At present, as I fix myself a coffee in the small kitchen of the townhouse that I share with Dear Olive, my dissertation is mocking me from the laptop I haul around like a chain, always dreading and half hoping that someone will rip it from my hands and run off, only to be caught later by the police when the thieves are found having died of boredom.

The sprinkler is on in the backyard and every few seconds it sprays the window. I wring my hands and shove them in my pockets, then take them out immediately and cover my face with them. Olive is at work. She is a doctor—the real kind, not the kind I'm slowing faking my way toward. We have a plan. The plan is to leave this tiny townhouse, and waste all my dad's money in a frivolous but possibly life-changing adventure ending with settling down in the country near the university I'll try my darndest to get a job at, and having the baby, now just a microscopic skeleton of DNA floating around in Olive, hopefully born to live without my happily perplexed expression on its face. Well Dad, we thought we'd start out in England, go to France, then maybe Spain, which I hear is fantastic, not that you would know because you've never really gone on a trip since you've always been here slaving away in the shop, which allowed all of us to do exactly what we wanted, but I'll be sure to send you a postcard. Having a wonderful time. The food is different, but the weather is hot. With Love From, your son, Dr. Dipshit.

His car pulls up and my heart jumps all over the place. I catch myself in the hall mirror. Oh dear, I say, we're sunk. The good news is that that stupid looking face won't be selling you paper at your favourite shop. I go downstairs and open the door.

"Hi, Son."

He grins and pulls me into a hug. I grin back and then hate myself for it. I'm a guy who everyone always gives chances to, and I feel now, with heavy authority, that I shouldn't be depended on at all, unless it's for disappointment. We go up the stairs, which strike me suddenly as being dirty and dammit I should have been vacuuming instead of taking a bath (See? See?), and I offer my dad a cup of tea, probably his third today.

Of course, that'd be great, he says. How's Olive, he says, still smiling. The warmth of his love has wriggled itself around my ankles and I feel stuck to my place on the floor, holding a teacup in one hand.

"She's pregnant. You're going to be a grandfather. I sold the business." I inhale and watch his face, watch this face I love and trust for signs of fury or annoyance or an expression that says, Why am I not surprised. Instead, he laughs and shakes his head quickly like he's stunned, he half raises his hands and laughs again. Then he does the right thing, of course he does, because he always does, and he comes around to where I'm stuck to the floor and then he laughs again and grabs me, hugging me again for the second time in minutes, the teacup stuck between us. Ha ha ha, he laughs, and takes the cup from my hands and takes charge and starts grilling me with questions. I kind of come to life finally, and guiltily, sheepishly, tell my dad of our plan that now (again) seems more delicate than my academic card house, but he's in, he's right in there thinking this is, "This is *exactly* why I wanted you to have it. This is so wonderful, wonderful."

There are people who in the same breath that they surprise you do exactly what you'd expect. With any luck, your father is that kind of person. It is late now, and he is gone. I haven't changed. I am still the same. I am wasting time, not vacuuming, not building a crib or making dinner. I am reading, but half-reading, half-looking up and staring and thinking that I just got another chance, don't screw it up. *You should really get up and do something.* I do get up, and I make Chicken L'Orange. I am a dad, and I am dependable, and I will do the right thing. The punchline arrives with Olive who comes home late, hungry and pregnant, and with one whiff of my spectacular dinner turns around, back where she came from, and throws up in the bushes. We have lettuce with no dressing, out on the porch, and she tells me to wipe that look off my face.

From Kentucky

I GOT YOU A NEW MUG FOR YOUR TEA. Well actually it was a gift from Nadine's brother the lawyer from Kentucky who doesn't like Shakespeare but thought the mug was funny. It says, 'The first thing we do, let's kill all the lawyers,' which is a quote from Shakespeare, Henry the Sixth, part two. It says so under the quote. It's a nice, deep grey colour and it's short with a big handle just like that Topflight one you always use. I'm drinking out of it now but I'll clean it out before I give it to you. Or maybe I'll just keep it here and it can be yours when you visit like the Topflight one.

I think you'd like Kentucky. It is like one huge hill that's pushed down in parts. You just keep rolling through it and it's like you can see it all at once—you can see the ranches that you will pass by in a half hour. You're at the top of a hill and then you drive down and pass barns and old fences with horses staring at you. From the snowstorm at home to Kentucky we felt the weather change, getting warmer and warmer and eventually we could drive with the windows open even though no Americans did. The trees had leaves, too, and we didn't even need our winter coats, even though Nadine packed enough sweaters for a season.

I think you'll like Nadine, but probably not her brother, not that it matters. I guess I'm just getting used to things. Nadine says there's nothing to get used to, it's perfectly normal, but I haven't had a girlfriend for thirty years so this isn't normal to me. At my age, as your grandfather would say, at my age I don't give a damn, I'll just say what I please. Mind you he was usually talking about the shape of women's breasts, or his digestion, or sex, or something, so that applies even more to me, who is pretty acceptable compared to him.

I stopped there and put the letter back in its envelope and lay my head on my pillow. I'd already read it once, when it came with the afternoon post, and it was about midnight now, but midnight boredom led me to reread letters. The window was open to the verandah and the night breeze was warm and carried the sounds of the Friday night city. I waved the envelope in front of my face. I had been sleeping, but on top of the bed, and not restfully, in a single bed in the furnished one room I rented from Madame Garner in her haphazard hotel. I kind of hated it, and had given notice in January that I was leaving to go to Belgium, but it was early April now and I hadn't gone, the short story being that I had no clean clothes and couldn't find someone to water my plants. The room was small and the furniture and decorations were old and girly—old-girly—a lot of lace and doilies and ornate frames with other people's—presumably Mme Garner's—families staring out disapprovingly. I figured these were to prevent me from having sex in the room, which I had had, but only once and it was so crappy, I'd put up with the awkwardness of other people's faces after that. I didn't invite people back. I felt like I hadn't had a girlfriend in thirty years either, and if I was exaggerating, I might as well say a hundred.

I turned onto my back and reached up with my foot, tipping the frame above me with a toe so that it hung crookedly, the old buttoned-up woman in the picture standing sideways. I swung my legs over the side of the bed and got up to close the window, but then didn't. Instead I walked out onto the verandah and leaned over the railing. A group of drunken guys were stumbling by, and I watched them punch each other and fall into doorways. They passed, and no one else walked by.

After my mother died, I left the cold. I decided belatedly, at the airport, actually, that the point was to start a new life somewhere else, but in the end I found that life was for the most part the same, although I was maybe more agitated, more alone, more of a stranger. A kind of sour variation. I didn't have anyone to accuse me of having changed and it was easier for that. Actual change, I think, is harder to do than everyone always says. I stepped off the plane and got my bags, and no one was there, of course, to pick me up and to ask what movie they had showed on the flight. I went to the airport bar and had a scotch, which is not my customary drink, but if I was trying things on new I might as well add scotch. The bar was dark and it stunk, and I was a little ripe myself, so I left. I bought a twisted roll, and took a taxi to Madame Garner's hotel and drank tea on the verandah.

Later that month I tried to meet people in the building, but was by far the youngest. Most of the rooms were occupied by vacationing retired couples—no one of that pre-married, post-school age that I was. The overhead fan ticked slowly in circles in the common room where others sat in pairs, or fours, playing cards. Sometimes I would go down in my slippers with a cigarette, and smile with no purpose at people with no need for my smile.

Eventually I met Louis. He was old and grumpy and self-conscious and shared my unsettled desire to be alone but to seek company, shared my strange sociability, that need to scowl at a friend. We often met at the front of the building. There was a bricked-over door to the left of the main entrance that must have once been the workers' entrance. We would sit on the unused steps and drink coffee, or gin, depending on the mood and time, and chat, or sit in silence, or sometimes fight like we knew each other better than we did. Sometimes Louis would storm off and I would throw my coffee cup at him, knowing that he loved theatrics.

"Do you want to see a trick?" he asked once, pulling out a deck of cards. I nodded. He asked me to shuffle the cards and cut the deck. I like shuffling—it's all I can do with cards—I can bend them back over themselves into a bridge, but can't get the coordination right, the finesse right, to cut the deck with one hand. A card jackknifed out of my grasp and flew into the street. Louis laughed and told me that I had stolen his trick, and I knew the moment was gone. He said, "that one's for the birds," and we watched some pigeons swoop down on the card, thinking it was food.

He had a broad face, his eyes were widely set and he had a

sort of straight line for a mouth. He reminded me, in his looks and demeanor, of a friend I had as a child, even though he was about thirty years my senior. He was, in fact, the same age as my father, and although they shared some odd traits like cheapness and a frustrating punctuality, which I chalked up to age, the two were very different. My father was very affectionate and open, and had recently started what seemed to be a new chapter in his life and so had a kind of rejuvenated optimism. Louis, on the other hand, was ornery and sarcastic, and one could never be sure if he was going to hug you or punch you, either of which followed by a nasty laugh forcing you to doubt his intentions. He enjoyed our friendship and was generous and helpful, even if it came off begrudgingly sometimes. And I sympathized with his general frustration, at times thinking that being stuck with him was a kind of retribution. He had an anxiety about his life, which I shared with him—we were both a little pissed off by our listlessness, not that we ever talked about it. And so we had found each other. And berated each other, consoled each other and sort of sought revenge on each other for what we saw as perhaps a little of an unjust pairing.

How much can I tell you about this time, down to the muscle and bone, how much of the loopy sadness? I know I'm not telling it. Louis, I knew, had secrets that spoiled him and left him in the shade for long stretches during which I would almost forget about him entirely. And the truth is, there wasn't anything *wrong*, nothing that couldn't be pinned down to misdirection and alcohol, just your average, run-of-the-mill dissatisfaction. But there I was, with the twitching eye and a 24-hour grimace. On both of us there was a tough and grizzly mark, scar tissue, no more or less than the others.

I decided to go out. It was a soft, light night, one that makes you want to get up when you wake in the middle of it; when I shut the door behind me I felt a rush of hope. I plodded past all the other rooms, down the stairs and into the night air. It was pretty quiet, despite being the end of the week, payday. I heard two cats fighting in an alleyway about a block over. I knew where Louis lived, which might surprise you. He wasn't a recluse, and actually kept a very nice apartment about fifteen minutes from my hotel. It had a dark façade in an alley, like a secret entrance, but when he opened the door, somehow it was always bright and always smelled inviting. He was a baker and he was baking now. I rapped on the wide wooden door.

"What the hell do you want?" He grabbed my shoulder and pulled me in. This made me smile and it occurred to me how much I depended on him, this sweet ogre. I put my jacket down on a bench by the door.

"I got a letter from my dad today. He says I would like Kentucky."

"You would, I guess. It's one of the best places in the world to drive through. Or live in. All hills. But God help you if you have to stop at a House of Waffles for something to eat. It's all shit unless you know someone there who can cook." Louis was from Kentucky. His family had a ranch there. After his parents died there was an ugly dispute over the question of which sibling should run the ranch with which children. Louis, who owned a third, had gladly taken leave of the responsibility, having no children of his own and considering himself of retirement age. He hadn't sold his share, but he didn't interfere either. Here, he sold his bread to local bakeries.

This kitchen included a huge oven and a long, wooden island covered with greased, circular stains and remnants of flour and hardened dough. I sat between two side tables, a lamp topped with a red lampshade, a shiny panther prowling on the base beside me.

"Why was he there?"

"They were checking out the House of Waffles."

A wry smile at this. "They?"

"He and his lady friend. Nadine."

"Nay-dene. Now there's a Kentucky woman. I probably know her."

That this ridiculous possibility had already occurred to me and had left me feeling uneasy didn't bear mentioning. The fact was, I figured any woman who knew my father and knew Louis would prefer Louis. My dad's K-way jackets and roadmaps, his shy deference to others, these things no match for the burly, whirling, roundhouse of a man like Louis.

"Well?" He put his hands on his hips. "So what d'ya want,

son?" Louis was in a great mood. He dusted his hands on his apron, patted a loaf with a big hand, a sign that he was done for now. I gave him a lopsided shrug and he rolled his eyes. He grabbed a six-pack of beer and a chunk of the steaming bread and split it in two, handing half to me for the road. He turned off the oven, shut the door behind us with a bang.

We were meandering through a now-dark city, a rambling conversation on our hands. Our solitude dogged us; we both felt comfortable but a little weird, a little low. We were talking about movies.

"Know who I love? Catherine Deneuve. She's more your generation, but I just love the way about her." I pictured her smoothing down her dress, holding her chin high.

"Did you know she was once chosen the Marianne of France?"

I didn't know what that was, which sort of embarrassed me.

"It's been the symbol, always a woman, of France—you know, a sign of the Republic, but it's respected by the working class and the stuffy bourgeois types. Since antiquity. Brigit Bardot was the Marianne once, and now it's some kid, I don't know who she is, but you'd know her. It's a bust, like a sculpture. We'll go see it one day." He paused and took a sip of beer, wiping his mouth. "But Catherine Deneuve was chosen once. It's quite an honour. Imagine being chosen by your country as a representative of all that's good about it? Voted in by the regular folks and the politicians? Now that's love." That seemed to me a strange remark to make. "Of course, it's always a woman. That's good, I think, that's it's a woman." What would a bust of Louis look like? I laughed at this to myself and got some beer up my nose. Louis turned. "What? What's wrong with me saying that?"

"Nothing, nothing. Just went down the wrong way, that's all."

He glared at me.

"Nothing, I said! Jesus."

"You think that we're all as enlightened and liberal as you. Well, I'm just making a comment that it's good it's a woman, you know, because where I come from—and where you come from, I might add—it would be some old white guy, so I'm just saying…"

My hand, which had been running along a rail, gave way suddenly to a rough, low barrier. Marked with orange high-visibility warnings, it was an old sewer tunnel being reclaimed for tourism. There were steps leading down to the forbidding darkness. I caught Louis's eye and began walking down. He stopped.

"Okay, yeah. This is a good idea."

The stairs were cold and dark and we had to feel our way into the tunnel through a hole we'd found in the wire fence. Pitch black. We held onto a wall and edged along. Was this a good idea? It was only dark, and sort of dank, there was no real danger that I could see. A test in blindness. Louis started singing "So Long, Marianne" behind me. I wanted to tell him to shut up. He pounded the wall with his palms, to the beat. I clung to the wall for sight. His voice rebounded around us. "Wouldn't it be good," he said, "if this were a path to another world? You know, like an escape to somewhere beautiful. Instead, you know, of being a tunnel for shit and piss."

"Like in *The Lion, the Witch and the Wardrobe*. Except this closet is a giant toilet."

"Exactly."

I was getting the hang of it now and didn't need to hold the wall. It was like skating for the first time. I began to walk away from the wall, at first just an arm's length away, reaching out to touch it periodically, reaching, reaching until I felt the roughness of the concrete quick against my fingertips. And then further away, until I was as good as in the middle of the street, the under-street of this place, trying to swing my arms naturally at my sides. And still I called back behind me as though something was on my mind, just to make sure I hadn't suddenly become alone. When do you think they're going to open this up? How do you think they cleaned this? And Louis started on about this or that, or made a joke because he couldn't get away from the shit jokes, being where we were.

After a while, I couldn't hear Louis behind me anymore. I felt blood rush to my mouth, and my ears roared, and I could have been down a chimney, or under water, or on top of a roof, for all the bearings I had. It was black—whatever adjusting my eyes had done, my sight was now reversed in quick-rising panic. I pivoted around and stood still for a second, arms out, legs bent as though at the ready for some kind of attack. Then I started to stumble back the way we had come, veering toward the wall. My voice gave me the creeps, bouncing around. And then I tripped on him.

Louis was lying with his legs splayed, partially propped up against the wall. I felt his head and shoulders, and shook him.

"Louis! Fuck, Louis! Wake up!" I felt my voice cracking. I almost grabbed his hair and banged his head against the wall. I leaned in close to his face. I thought I saw it: An eye opening. His mouth cracking into a crooked smile.

"Ha ha. I'm not that old," he said.

I don't really know what happened then. Sometimes I think I kicked him hard in the side. He struggled and got up and got a hold of my collar and punched me in the mouth, knocking me back. We tumbled and told each other off and said some really awful things, cruel personal accusations, and then I ran out. I heard a hollow laugh coming down the tunnel. Turning toward it, part of me felt I should go back. Hoist him up, dust ourselves off, follow that tripwire of our friendship out into the light. But I turned around again and kept going.

I never saw Louis again. It wasn't hard not to run into each other, both of us being as we were, although for a while I thought I saw him everywhere, mostly in my mind, inside that tunnel. At first, it just felt like one of the many dry periods of our friendship. I brushed off the ache as temporary, but sometimes I feel it still. Years went on, and we never bumped into each other. When the tunnel became a finished tourist spot, I lined up to pay, then followed other people into the well-lit, civilized underworld. When I stopped unexpectedly at a particular spot, touching the wall, a child bumped into me and let go of the balloon he was holding. It floated to the low ceiling, and he stood waiting for me to pull it down.

I moved out of the hotel and found a small storefront that had been converted into a studio. Actually, it used to be a bakery, and the smell of bread was long a reminder of Louis, but then, eventually, just of itself, and now when I smell fresh bread I think of that studio. One night I got up and tried to make a loaf in the old defunct oven. The smell that came out of there was worse than those sewer tunnels; something must have died in there. I stayed for a year and then moved elsewhere, casting a line of more responsible decisions, each place more practical than the last, each further from home but closer to permanence.

Once, at a party—unusually sober and talking to a girl that I would eventually take back home with me, eventually to Kentucky, to the hills and valleys, with a packed lunch between us and a map to Nay-dene's brother's house—I looked over the girl's shoulder and noticed a box in the corner of the room with a lamp sticking out of it. It had a red shade and a black panther on the base.

It reminds me of something. One summer when I was young, I found an injured crow in our backyard. It seemed to me its wing was hurt because it could only fly short distances and was visibly frustrated that it could not get up to the top of our fence. Its friends or enemies were calling to it from the trees as it hopped to and fro in front of the fence, making a strained call of its own. I wondered if it could live on the ground instead, if the other birds would fly away and leave it there. I left food and water, and one day I went out and it was gone. I don't know if it got up to the fence, if it flew away, or if in fact it toppled over the other side, into the brush—the best it could do.

Wedding Day

I DIDN'T TAKE TO PARENTHOOD like anything takes to water. I took to it slowly and clumsily and much less joyfully than I was expected to. I took to it like one toe at a time into a freezing lake, methodically and seriously. And because I had to, not in any poor-me sense but in oh-shit responsibility, and now I have a feeling that that's what lots of people do. I know there are people who were born to parent—'born mothers'—but I'm most suspicious of these. I uncurled the baby's fingers and stared at his hands as though tiny hands might tell me the thing I needed to know. And then, like getting used to the water, I started to like it. If no one rushed me, if no one splashed me, I could get used to it, moving my arms and staying afloat, just so.

Those hands would reach for mine and I felt like we were saving each other.

He wasn't a baby anymore, and when I watched him marry it wasn't with sadness, but with relief, with calm. I sighed deeply and felt proud and happy and I smoothed down my beige, satin, mother-of-the-groom uniform with a nice hand-wiping feeling of *There. Done.* The organ pounded out the final movement, and we rose.

On the way out of the church, the minister reminded me of the Women's Guild meeting that week. I'd missed the last one, and subsequently had brought some quickly-made tuna sandwiches for a funeral a day late. The doors of the church had been locked and I'd almost left the sandwiches on the steps, but I worried that the more responsible women of the Guild would recognize my plate, ill-timed holder of sandwiches. Ken and I had had the tuna sandwiches for dinner. He told me no one was hungry at a funeral anyway.

I pulled into the driveway behind two cars that had beat me home. The door was unlocked and I could hear conversation from the kitchen. I looked in the direction of the master bedroom and paused, but put my keys on the parson's bench by the door and joined the din.

"Wasn't that lovely? Oh, Madeline, that was lovely, really." My two sisters and my brother were uncovering sandwiches and making punch and opening pickle jars and whipping up dip.

"Ken would have loved it," my other sister chimed. Yes, I nodded, and handed her a plate of vegetables. My brother grabbed a carrot stick as it passed, and for a moment he was fourteen, not forty-four. He was opening wine bottles; he blew out his cheeks and looked around in mock exasperation when I caught his eye. I laughed.

When I was young and my mother would host Christmas or Thanksgiving or Easter dinners, and our relatives would come over, I often got dizzy and wanted to lie down. I loved my relatives and wanted to see them, and couldn't explain my desire to be alone. Everyone was so caring and inquisitive and attentive. But I would get instantly tired. "She's rundown, poor thing," my aunt or grandmother or mother would say, and I would go to my room and stare out the window. I might lie down and sleep, then be woken for turkey, red pillow mark on my face. Today I felt a bit like that, or I felt it coming on—the desire to sneak away. I shook it off, though. Brushed my hands through my hair and smiled brightly, opening my arms for congratulatory hugs.

I won't tell it all to you. You've seen a wedding reception before, probably twenty, like me. It was loud and fun and bright and everyone was full and drunk by the end, which was early, by the couple's request. They had a last dance to "Wild Horses" and then a cab came to take them to the airport. People left. A few old friends stuck it out in a corner of the backyard.

I sat on the couch in the cool quiet of the living room. I took off my beige strappy shoes and massaged my feet. I lay my head back against the pillows and gazed out the window at the upper branches of an old tree. I'd planted it myself years ago, and with a new gardener's short-sightedness had put it too close to the house. Its branches often wipe against the glass. They were doing that now.

Someone was trying to open a door while holding something. Evrin emerged clutching two gin-and-tonics. Evrin is my oldest friend. More like a sister to me than my own sisters, and looks more like me, too. We are two who are never apart, from grade school until now. People confused us, always asked about the other. There had been tearful spats and fierce competition in our youth. *Don't get Mad, get Evrin*, her campaign posters for student council read, something I'd tried out for only because she did. Dance classes, sports, university, later the same neighborhood, houses apart just like we'd planned. We'd wanted our children to marry. Evrin had a son as well, who had come out years ago; my son was not his type. And my son had found his Jane. And now here we were. Evrin put the glasses down and eased onto the couch.

"Another one bites the dust."

"Who was that woman crying so hard at the ceremony?" Neither of us had cried, had instead grinned stupidly at one another. I didn't know who the crier was, but her sniffling had gotten to me somehow.

Laughter sailed through the open windows, reminding me of parties at our parents' houses during which we would steal off for the night, abdicating our hors d'oeuvres duties. It was dark and cool here in the room, with the feeling of heat held at bay. Rain was not far off, rain that would bring relief and send hangers-on running for their coats and purses, goodbye kisses and offers to help clean up. In the kitchen were stacked serving trays, a garbage bag full of paper plates, champagne gone flat. I could hear the dog sniffing around in there, chomping on the odd grape or cheese cube.

"You know what I would like?"

"No. What?"

"A cold dunk. I never have cold baths, because baths should be hot. And neither of us have a pool. And there's no lake. And

all I want is to dunk in some cold water."
"I can spray you with the kitchen tap."
"Maybe it'll rain."

It did rain. It rained and rained, rain pounding on the skylights like nails. Ken's old college roommate slipped on the deck and nearly toppled his huge self into the garden. With no real warning except for the change in air pressure and the sudden clouds, people scattered and bumped into each other. Evrin and I watched them from the window and laughed. A flea circus.

"A flea wedding!" said Evrin, and did a little imitation of what we saw to the tune of a high-pitched circus song. My drink went up my nose, hers sloshed on the floor. Later my feet stuck to the spill, and I took a few days to mop it up.

Evrin was on drying duty, and as she dried, I took leave from the kitchen. I walked leisurely down our hall, my finger trailing on the wood siding, and allowed myself token nostalgia when passing my son's room. This was not the first time I had snuck off. I opened the master bedroom door and closed it behind me. I sat on the edge of the bed.

"Hi."

I stroked Ken's forehead with the backs of my fingers. His eyelids fluttered, slowly, and he turned his head to a glass of water beside him. I handed it to him and he drank.

"Everyone still here?"

"No. The kids wanted to get off early, so most people left after them. The Browns stayed and so did Rick and Marilyn, but now they're gone. Ev and I are cleaning up." I looked out the window to see what he could see from the bed. "It's raining." He pulled me in for a kiss.

"Rain? That's got nothin' on snow." He stroked my arm. We were quiet.

Ken looked so different now; sometimes I caught myself staring. His gaunt face and thin arms proved how disloyal the body can be. He was looking at me with kindness. I rearranged his pillows. My hands lingered on the fitted sheet beneath him and I fought off the urge to get in there with him. He gave me a smile and told me to tell Evrin to go easy on the gin. I closed the door quietly.

When I was young, my father was always ill. He was pills and clean sheets and poisoned sleep, and then he was gone. Before his death he was a presence, part of the smell and sound of the house. Pillowy and medicinal, it was for him that I was reminded to be quiet, to refrain from slamming doors, never to yell. I envied children who had loud, electric games with whistles and sirens. I glided around the house in stockinged feet, a master of creakless door-opening. I brought boiled eggs, tea and a salt shaker on a small tray and would practice leaving it on his bedside table without his hearing me. Sometimes I would sneak in and watch him, pretend he was dead, and would scare myself so much I would wake him up in a panic. He wanted to be the one to sign off on my schoolwork, assembly forms, trip forms, tests. His was the signature that charted my early school years, and the first day my mother had to sign something, I cried. Loopy and feminine, her name had none of the power and protection of my father's scrawl. I became latently quiet in a loud adult world.

Evrin was putting away the dishes, humming a jazzy "Here Comes the Bride."

When I met Ken, he was fair and sporty, carrying a tennis racquet like another arm. But he was pale and frail as well—a weakness just under the skin, over the bones—and it wasn't long after our wedding that he began to get sick, and had the first in a series of many diagnoses, followed over the years with remissions and tests and rediscoveries and removals of growth. This was my territory, sickness. Its poisonous comfort drew me in.

On our wedding day, the city endured its biggest snowstorm ever. You might remember it: Everything shut down for a week, except the stock market. Like the desert, or a bombed-out city, "or Moscow!" my father said: Everything from trees to swing sets to houses were obscured. Men's hats flew into the air like untied balloons. Afterward, stories of bravery and survival on the soggy front pages of the week-overdue papers: Families trapped in buried cars listening to people walk overtop of them on the packed snow. Horns honking underfoot.

The only people who attended our wedding, my parents' house its new location, were the ones who were already there:

Stranger-relatives, my mother and assorted others. Two cousins near my age that I hadn't seen in ten years, Buxom Beth and Sallow Sal, I had thought to myself at the time. They were twins, but nothing in their appearance or demeanor suggested it. Beth had the burden of big breasts, which had developed before her personality had, and she depended on them for attention, and, I suspected, for her livelihood, which seemed a little vague but was linked to a coquettish smile, which she pointed in the direction of the priest. Her brother compensated for her brazenness by attempting to blend into the wallpaper; he declined any offers of food or drink. Ken's uncle Dick and his dancer-wife Tango Jolie (who also made her profession with her lovely body, but took in it such an indisputable pride that I was more worried about something happening to her on the icy steps, should we leave the house, than myself) were there. In the upstairs room, Ken's brother Nick; charming, colourful, fabulously dressed, eyeing the priest. Father Peter had passed out the night before, as the snow fell, after just one more glass of sherry. My mother had been forced to negotiate the pullout under the sleeping clergyman, a task that left her blushing. She held up limbs as I opened the bed, keeping the silence. My mother dried morning dishes and kept a brave face, preparing for the indoor storm that was sure to occur once I discovered the state of the outside world. Lastly, Evrin, who had been invited to stay over to calm my last-minute jitters. She woke me like a child on Christmas morning, gazing out the window with her palms on the glass. "Holy. Shit. Mad, what a day for a wedding."

Ken wasn't there. He slugged it out in the *four-feet-high-and-rising* snow to get there. But first, of course, he went to the church, in the opposite direction. By the time the soaking, freezing and almost translucent Ken arrived at my parents' household, lubricated as it was with Morning Glories and rum and coffee, a cheer went up at the sight of him. The groom was there, the wedding was on.

The night was a dream, both snowy and foggy, a fire in the fireplace and clothes on the radiator filling the room with moist comfort. Tango Jolie and Nick did the twist, Father Peter engaged Sal in a loud one-sided conversation about baseball,

Beth pinned Dick up against the fridge, a toothpick in her teeth. Ken and I fell into our wedding bed, my childhood bed, the room in the turret, the new world swirling with snow.

The morning our son was born—the morning Geoff was born—Ken was in the hospital too. He was having a tumour removed, two floors above me, and when Evrin shouted at me to do it for Ken, I looked up at the panelled ceiling and tried my very best.

As I held the wrinkled Geoff in my hands they passed me the phone. It was Ken. What do you do when you're always a room away? When you have to settle for static and recall? Ken laughed, and said, "He looks just like you."

Here was the man for whom I was prepared to glide, silent for the sleeping, but he wouldn't let me. Ken loved noise. He wired stereo speakers into the walls during a healthy hiatus. Noise piped into our rooms, under our sheets, the soundtrack to a delicate love delicately played: Radio shows, ballads, audio books, opera, jazz. When he could, we would dance. "Relax, Mad. Why can't you *relax?*" I would laugh and try to shake it out, wiggling my arms like a rubber band. Just trying to shake it out.

Geoff didn't look like me at all. He was Ken, through and through. None of my dominant genes persevered—no dark eyebrows, black hair, black eyes. Geoff was sunny and blond and grew to look hauntingly like a young Ken. Funny and gregarious, Geoff became what I wasn't. He dove into things that I avoided; he took charge but also took heart; he had become a man whom I knew already. I watched him slide into home base, and as the dust settled around us I knew he was like Ken in all but one respect: Geoff was uncanny in his health. This miniature man grew strong and solid while I separated pills and waited for results. Now he was the marrying age, and I could count on one hand how often Geoff had been sick. Never a broken bone, or a sprain, or a fracture for those smooth and sporty limbs. He had been in hospitals only to visit, and to doctors only as routine.

Jane and Geoff were at the precipice of something new, and in a hallway photograph they looked eager and fresh-faced— looking just outside the frame, untouched by hard weather and late nights. I had a sort of sick feeling, something sad and full of longing. And then I heard breaking glass.

"Sorry, Mad. It just slipped from my hands." The rain still pounded against the windows and I could hear my tree's branches, crying like windshield wipers. I crouched and lifted a shard of glass, champagne snaking across the floor.

Fall

SEPTEMBER

"Gimme your hands, flat out, like this. No, like this."

I put out my hands, palms down, and my sister Effie hammers on them with her own. "You're s'posed to move them, stupid." I am supposed to move them. What a rube I am. "What a rube you are. R-U-B-E. Rubus Majora."

"Shhh, you two!"

We bring our hands down to our sides and look ahead. Then I poke Effie with a needley finger. We are outside the entrance of the church—not outdoors, but in the narthex, lining up to go into the church proper. We aren't Catholic. Well, no, I supposed we are, now. We aren't "Returning Catholics"—the kind welcomed by the sign with the movable letters out front. "Welcome Back, Returning Catholics." We are Brand New Catholics. Converts.

I am the nervous boy in starchy white button-down and grey wool pants, already scratching. Effie is wearing a cream-coloured dress and carrying a boxy plastic purse with Minnie Mouse on the front, bulging with so many dolls that it just barely closes with its click-snap lock.

We were Protestant originally. Our mother was, anyway. Effie and I have never been to church at all until this summer. Our mum decided to convert after our father left last year. We are welcome here, by some. I get extra big smiles from some ladies. They feel sorry for us. Other times I know that kids my age are staring, trying to figure out what makes us different, because I guess someone told them we are. Our parents haven't gotten divorced, so I suppose that is okay for those hung up on the rules, but really that's only because no one knows where he is (*poor dear*). Our mother had always wanted to be Catholic —I'd overheard her telling our aunt on the phone—because it is more mysterious and romantic than Protestantism. Effie has been calling me "The Gen-u-flec-tor" all summer.

On our first excursion to Mass, back at the beginning of summer, Effie pleaded to be allowed to bring a small doll in her pocket. It would make her 'more comfortable,' she begged. She convinces our mother of many things by speaking her language, which mainly consists of variations on the word Comfort since our dad left. During Mass, she played with the doll on the pew. By the end of the summer, she finagled a whole purse full of dolls and clothes and little plastic shoes, and she roots through the collection during sermons, making the dolls nod their little heads during the chant-like recitation of the Confiteor.

I confess to Almighty God,
and to you here present,
that I have sinned through my own fault,
["mea culpa, mea culpa, mea maxima culpa"]
in my thoughts and in my words,
in what I have done and in what I have failed to do.
And I ask Blessed Mary, ever Virgin,
all the Angels and Saints,
and you here present
to pray for me to the Lord, our God.

"So what did you confess to, Avi?" my mother asks me. We are walking back to the car.

"Nothing. —Ow!" I rub my arm. Effie giggles.

"Well, I suppose confession is a private ritual, you don't have to tell me..."

"Then why do you keep asking me?"

"...Just as long as you're not actually confessing to nothing."

Effie, counting on fingers, says, "I confessed to hitting Avi, kicking Vanessa Smyth, saying JESUSCHRIST—" she glances at our mother "—in vain and for thinking that Father Brian looks stupid in a dress."

"Effie, don't tell *Father Brian* that! It's not a dress, it's a robe."

"But I thought we were *supposed* to tell him everything."

I really like the confession booth. It is dark and close and quiet. Not that I do any actual confessing. It isn't that I am against it, or that I don't think I've done anything wrong—I always feel guilty and bad about all kinds of things—but I think Father Brian doesn't want to hear that. I just sit there in the quiet. Father Brian sits there too. Eventually I smile at him through the grate. My dad and I had a number of comfortably silent discussions. Part of me wonders if the "broken home" thing is the reason Father Brian allows me to partake in this silent confessional.

Father Brian is about my father's age, in his forties. He is handsome and rugged-looking. I imagine that the girls have crushes on him—not that Effie is a gauge for this sort of thing. She is right now preoccupied with swearing and inflicting pain, and approaches her misbehavior with an almost scientific-like curiosity. *Swearing in front of mother yields bad reaction, unless quoting someone else swearing, which proves less severe. Interesting.* Her tales from the confessional involve an enthusiastic recounting of past swears and beatings. As for me, my silent confessions continue with Father Brian for some time, and my mother continues to hound me about what I've said, extensive confessions expected from a son who will never say more than "fine" when asked how his school day went.

OCTOBER

Mass is finished and I am behind the brown and musty curtain that divides my meetings with Father Brian from the rest of the world. I get comfortable, clear my throat and lean back. I close my eyes during these visits, but I don't doze off. I just soak it in. All the brown, brown wood, brown chair, brown curtain with little balls on it, brown grate.

"I've been having doubts about my faith."

I open my eyes. "Oh."

"Particularly, I mean, with the Trinity. Not that this means anything to you, probably, but—" I hear him cross himself. "Lately—this is so ridiculous—I just can't believe it. I can't believe *in* it. I mean, I know that it is so very basic, but I have reached some kind of standstill."

"Oh."

I pick at some lint on my pants. We sit in silence for a while. I hear Father Brian lean back and exhale. I get up clumsily, give an over-happy, nonsensical smile to the empty grate where his face had been, and leave the booth.

My mother is cutting my hair. The scissors snip and cut around my eyes, which squeeze shut, and my ears, which can't. She stands back to look. My bangs are getting shorter and shorter with every attempt at evenness.

"What did you have to say to Father Brian today in confession?"

"That I have been having doubts about my faith."

"Avi. I didn't know you had faith in the first place."

"Mmm. Yes, especially worried about the trinidy." She sits down on a chair opposite me, looks me hard in the eye, and then gets up again and dries my hair roughly with a towel.

Lord, I am not worthy to receive you, but only say the word, and I shall be healed.

Mass is over. I thought it would never end and then hoped it wouldn't. I run my hand along the pews. I pause to tighten my shoelace, and then head over to the booth. I feel like I'm at a magic show—that when I pull the curtain, half a woman will be stretched out inside. I sit down and am aware of Father Brian's profile.

"My mum says it's like water, the trinidy."

"Avi, look. I'm sorry about what I said last week. I don't know what came over me. We should—"

"No, listen. And so, water, see, can be regular liquidy water, and it can be ice, and it can be steam. You know. Like, three things."

"Yes, I know."

"So what's the problem, then? You have to have blind faith, you know." I got this bit from my mother, who I imagine suffers from the same dilemma. I feel quite removed, having never really thought I had faith to lose.

"Yes, I know. I know that, Avi. You're right, of course. I can see you've been paying attention."

"Listen." I turn and peer at him through the grate. He keeps his face turned in profile, but his eyes twitch in my direction. "No, I haven't been listening. Well, yes. Yes, sure I have. But this is, like, the *basic* part of it. I mean, do you think I don't think it's weird that we eat bread and pretend it's a body? I'd rather it just be bread, not that I can even understand the body stuff. Let alone the blood thing. But you have to *fake* it, you know? I bet half the people here fake it because that helps them believe it more." Effie, and her faithful, nodding dolls. My mother, singing every hymn with her eyes wide open and bright.

"Yes. But don't you think that's a bit of a tall order? Or just wrong? We pretend to understand, and base our beliefs on something we don't really buy into." I can tell he's sort of talking to himself now. He seems to be looking down at his lap. I knock on the grate with my fingers.

"Hey! Sure it is. Sure. But, I mean, we can't prove it like you can prove the dinosaurs or something. Sometimes you just have to hope that something is the way you want it to be so that you feel better. You know what I mean?"

"Of course. That's what *I* mean, though, Avi. Maybe we should be facing ourselves instead of putting everything on a hope or a belief that we think is a little suspicious anyway." He sort of smiled and shook his head.

NOVEMBER

"Look," I say, rushing into the booth and pulling the curtain behind me, "I know that you think you shouldn't be doing this if your faith is failing you, but maybe that's just—"

I start, looking at the grate. Father Andrew. I sink onto the stool. Old, awful, nosy Father Andrew.

"Father Brian is away today. Come down with a bit of a cold, I'm afraid. It is so damp, Avi, isn't it? Weren't you taught the proper way to begin a confession, Avi?"

My face burns. It feels like I'm watching myself on television.

"Forgive me, Father, for I have sinned." I make up something.

Something about lying to my mother.

I don't go to Confession the next week. The following Sunday also slips by without my visit to the box. I hide around the corner, scuffing my shoes on the linoleum and watching Father Brian's under the curtain. I have no idea if he has gotten into any trouble as a result of our meetings—his shoes give no indication—some kind of brutal adult-version of the lashings I've heard about from the more mischievous boys of the church. I also stop talking to my mother about things, due mainly to lack of material, which she attributes to some kind of dark, teenaged identity crisis. This suits me fine.

DECEMBER
It is cold, and I hug myself as I circle around to the back of the Church. I told my mother I'd walk home after Mass, as she and Effie and most of the other churchgoers got into their cars and headed home for warmth and fruitcake and afternoon TV. I head for the chestnut trees in the churchyard beside the parking lot. I have taken to looking for chestnuts, their empty casings interesting, but the whole chestnuts *in* their spiky shells are the prizes. I collect as many as I can find, and stand at the edge of the fence whipping them at far off gravestones in the cemetery, trying to outshoot myself and watching the nuts explode on concrete crosses.

I have barely gotten to the edge of the parking lot when I hear my name.

"Avi!"

Father Brian waves me over to the side of the church. I blush in spite of the cold, and start walking toward him. He is standing beside a ladder, which goes all the way up the brick wall to the black church bell. When he talks, I can see his breath.

"I need a hand. We want to ring the bell on Christmas Day like we always do, but something seems to be jammed in there. I'm going to climb up the ladder and see if I can dislodge it, but I need someone to hold me steady from here. Are you in a rush, or do you have a minute?"

I say I can do it, sure. I rest a mittened hand on the side of the ladder as Father Brian looks up. He claps me on the back, gives me a smile, and starts to climb. I take his place in front of the ladder and grip it with both hands, watching him move upward. The ladder nudges against the wall with every step. Father Brian reaches as close as he can to the church bell, and I squint in the winter sun. The wind has unravelled his scarf and it whips crazily around his head as he stretches his arm up into the old black bell. I hold fast to the ladder, my fingers aching. He dislodges what was inside the bell with a jerk, and the ladder wobbles. Then it rights itself. Father Brian holds the thing in his hand and lifts his face into the sun. My ears are freezing, but I fight the urge to cover them. And then he falls. The ladder suddenly becomes lifeless without his weight, his arms windmill in a cartoonish silhouette against the sun, and then he plunges in an arch away from the church wall. I am partially aware of a Frisbee that begins to fall with him, then catches some air and soars up in the opposite direction toward the trees.

I am waiting for the ambulance. Father Brian is crying. I am sitting with my mittened hand on his shoulder. One of the altar boys who saw what happened and called the ambulance is now inside getting blankets or doing something else helpful. We're alone. Half on the grass and partway into the bushes. Father Brian's whimpers seem so loud and I feel sick listening to him. I brush my hand over his hair and gently stroke his shoulder. I stop when I hear the sirens.

After Bingollo's

I HEARD THAT THERE IS NOTHING WORSE than to lose a child. This is what I'd heard, and I nodded my head stupidly with when-can-I-change-the-topic compassion, my hands in my pockets, jangling my keys. But there is. There is something worse than a parent losing a child and that is me, losing my child.

I would wake mornings and remember, comprehension like a punch, like a sucker-punch. And then, still, years later. You still get that second, though, when you first wake, you're happy, a ten-year-old, and maybe the sun is hitting your face just so.

I didn't lose my child. My wife did. She had that minute of misaligned sight, that lapse, that momentary relaxation. A child, my child, is gone. She did it. Her. Feeling her pockets for pruning sheers, laughing over the fence. Forgetting the small pink body, the body slipping silently under the water, watch how long I can hold my breath. Silence like a waiting room, under the water, filling ears, dimming thoughts. How long can we hold our breath now? I've been holding mine for years. But sometimes it comes out in bursts, in great gulps of anger and curse and accusation. And just when you would be right to think I am the world's biggest ass, she does leave. Not many people will take blame with their grief. Her note had only one word on it and I didn't believe it, but there it was and I was alone. I pulled all the junk, all the glasses and mail off our counter in a rage and it stayed there for three days, coffee filling the grout in the floor, because who's going to clean it up? The saddest geography teacher in the world. I could mark myself with a pin on a pull-down map. What's this, kids? The saddest geography teacher, Sir.

Yessir. The glass door closes behind me and smoke rushes my face. I am in Bingo Country, now. Here on a recommendation from a friend who had not only won three hundred dollars, but said that bingo was great for a laugh, get out of the house and why not meet her there. The dark Chevys of Bingollo's Bingo Hall. I had trouble finding a spot, it is that crowded.

It's never something nice when you overhear someone talking about you, which makes one question humanity, really. *You know, not to be mean, but him losing that kid was the best excuse he ever had to keep being a grumpy asshole.* It's not true. Who needs an excuse, is what I wanted to say, when there are people like YOU. I'm in pain. I'm just shy. I'm an introvert. I hate Bingo already and where the hell is my friend. The look that pisses everyone off is on my face. I get myself a card and a stamper, with a smile to a woman with Loreen on her name tag, who says to me, "Good luck, hon."

Bingollo's Bingo Hall. It is large, packed with fold-out tables turned every which way. The ceiling is high and the smoke drifts up, a cloud hanging beneath the yellowed tiles. The announcer, or caller, I'm not sure what they're called—bingo crier—perches in a glass box positioned above our heads, like a quarantined lifeguard. Old stickers are pasted all over the glass. Between hauls off her own cigarette, she calls out the numbers from a rotating contraption in front of her. She exhales and says the number at the same time, and the smoke comes out shaped like a G-10. Really.

Loreen asks me to keep moving, she has a lot people in line if I don't mind. Well, don't you know it, this is the busiest spot in town. I choose a prime seat about a third of the way deep into the tables, four people in. A man with no less than a half dozen cards in front of him is quickly stamping as the numbers are called. He raises his eyes and nods, mid-stamp. He takes in my one card, and pegs me for a novice. I look at my card, with its brightly coloured letters and numbers, for clues of how I ended up in such a fine establishment. I catch eyes with a woman about twenty years my senior. She turns away and loses herself in a hacking cough. Loreen calls out B-10. I have B-9.

I play my card, and then buy another. And another. One has to take this sort of thing slow, get the moves down. I play four, and then I meet the man in front of me. Gerry. And his buddies, Cliff and Dicky and Herm. They're all in their late sixties, early seventies, well scrubbed and lively and punchy, a whiff of aftershave. They snort and groan at each other's quips and jokes, and beg Herm to stop that infernal racket. He's been crooning old drinking songs, old Nova Scotia songs, old man songs. Herm's a tenor, a clear voice, someone who has sung the same songs for thirty years. I am enjoying myself, sort of, reservedly sharing in their fun with the odd remark. The ladies at the next table call out, Keep it down, because they can't hear the numbers with all the noise. Cliff raps on the table and asks what Dicky thinks this is, a bingo hall? The ladies roll their eyes.

When the evening is over, we push back our chairs and stand to stretch. Gerry looks me over.

"If you came here to pick up chicks you could have at least shaved. Jesus. You look like you used an old bus ticket. You a widower?" He is looking at my ring finger, with its pale indentation.

"No."

"Kids?"

"No."

"We're all widowers. The merry widowers. Except Dicky, he's a crabby bastard."

"Me too."

People are gathering their purses and coats. The woman from the Bingo cage is climbing down a ladder, cigarette hanging from her lips.

"Well."

Gerry smooths himself down and looks at his friends.

"Would you like to join us for a beer? At Herm's. We do it every week. God knows those hens drive a man to drink."

My house. Full of empty picture frames, no one to repopulate them. Foul, unwashed coffee mugs on the table beside my easy chair. Milk gone off.

Yes, that would be nice.

"It's pretty tricky getting to Herm's old bachelor pad," Gerry tells me.

The ride to Herm's is more than tricky. At one point I think this might be some elaborate joke, that Gerry, Cliff, Dicky and Herm are going to corner me, rob me and leave me in my car, lost. The roads wind, and save for Cliff's headlights in my rearview mirror, it is pitch black. Gerry fiddles with the radio for an alarming number of minutes. Normally I would have lost my patience, but instead I feel grateful to him. His rough and clean presence in the car is a rare comfort.

He is jovial, busy, a mayorish sort of man's man, a lady's man, a man about town. Has lost his wife to Alzheimer's, that stranger-maker. She was the life of the party, Gerry says, a real looker. An actress, big in Winnipeg before they moved to St. Stephen's two decades ago now. Lit up the stage like a firefly, and could she dance!

Gerry laughs. "She would whirl and get whirled around that stage, and when she walked, boy," Gerry waggles his finger at me, "she was like what Jack Lemmon says about Marilyn in *Some Like it Hot*, like Jell-O on springs!" He shakes his head sadly. His Jell-O-spring wife. He perks up, now, turning to me. "I run a bookstore-pub around here. It's called Bev's. After her. Bev. You know it?"

"No," I say, hoping he won't take offence. He can't imagine how little I know anymore.

"Oh. Well, no matter. You should come sometime. I only have the best books, *and* the best beer on tap. No crap." He reaches into his jacket and pulls out a paperback.

"Have you read this?"

"What is it?"

He clucks and leaves it on the armrest between us with a loving pat.

"*Cat and Mouse*, Günter Grass. It's yours."

This touches me, and makes me uncomfortable. I laugh nervously.

"Thanks. Thank you. I'll, uh, give it back to you when I'm done."

Gerry laughs at this.

Suddenly, in front of me, I see two large, glassy eyes catching the headlights. A dog. This is all I see and then it all happens too fast. The car lurches.

"Oh God. Oh Jesus Christ."

And we are stopped.

I fumble and open the door and run roadside around the back of the car, holding my arms up to Cliff's headlights. There is high grass at the side of the road and my stomach tightens. My eyes are slowly adjusting to the darkness. I walk to the front door of the car, adrenaline rushing in my ears, and kneel down beside the dog, its leg twitching. It is a large German Shepard, no collar, but well fed. I squeeze my eyes shut and then open them in time to see a watery glance up in my direction. The eyes stare forward and the dog goes dead. I push my thumb knuckles into my own eyes.

"He's a sensitive boy. Poor guy's all shook."

I hear Cliff's door slam and he and Herm and Gerry walk over.

"Aw, no," Cliff says, and turns away.

"Just like ol' Julie, eh Ger?"

"Yeah. Hopefully she didn't suffer."

"Happier now," said Herm.

I want to turn on them and laugh outright at this lie. I can feel myself steeling up, straightening up, lacing and bracing myself against kindness. I hate niceties, how sympathy blows off when the wretched are left to their business. I look up at a dark house with one light glowing in a front window.

"I, uh, should go up there and let those people know."

"Okay."

"I'll be back in a few minutes."

"Okay, son." I falter at this. I start to go, but then turn back to Gerry.

"Remember when I told you I had no kids?" He says nothing. "I do. I did. I had a daughter."

I reach the house and stand on the border of a well-tended garden. I look around, down the hill, and see my headlights stretched out on the road like a reminder. I see the mens' silhouettes. They look like they have stopped to jump-charge my car. I cannot see the dog. I ring the bell and wait for the sound of someone coming to the door. *Who could that be?* I see a man about my height through the smoked glass. There is a young boy behind him in the doorway of another room, peering at me, biting the sleeve of his pajama top.

We are making our way down the steep hill, the man and I. I can tell he is upset enough to cry, but doesn't want to, not in front of me. The boy doesn't know. I had asked the man to come outside so I could tell him about the dog. The news will be broken to the boy with quiet kindness, which is impossible. He will always remember this night because of me.

"What was her name?"

"Shadow."

That queen of dog names. I hesitate. I pat him on the back awkwardly. He tightens his mouth into a forced smile.

I'm sorry.

I can see the men from here, standing slightly apart but all looking up toward the house, arms at their sides, each singular, like cedars in the dark.

Paper Girl

SHE WAS A JAZZY, HUSKY BOY-GIRL in tweed pants and ruffled blouses, blouses with buttons at the back, which someone else has to do up, pearly, toothy, button-by-button. Often a hard-to-reach middle-of-the-back patch of her freckled skin winked at the sun. She smoked and cut her own hair. Badly. A cowboy/cancan combo, our newspaper girl, and because of her I became an avid follower of world events. I showered before seven o'clock and started wearing cologne. I was fifteen.

Nora—God, her name killed me—rode a twelve-speed bike with a white metal basket full of papers in front and two saddlebags full behind. She took her time bringing the news to our sleepy street—dragged lazily on cigarettes, and scuffed her shoes on the sidewalk to slow herself down. I would wait for her, watch her coming along the street like she was arriving for a shoot-out at ten paces.

"Hey!" she'd grin at me. "Here!"

Usually I didn't catch the paper and it landed with a paper splat on the porch. My gut clenched in a happy knot.

She was a little older than me. She didn't go to my school. I figured she didn't go to school at all, but lived on top of a piano in a nightclub. The truth is I didn't really know much about her, just her name, because I overheard my mom ask her once.

Late summer has a kind of sadness that comes with the counting down of days, even though fall is the best season.

I was filling the old steel whistling kettle at the kitchen sink, our split bungalow with its kitchen upstairs, overlooking an upper deck my dad had built. His homemade birdhouses and the squirrels that lived in them. My parents were at friends' cottage; *cottage whoring*, my dad called it. I heard the slap of a paper on our neighbour's porch and hustled downstairs to the door, aware of my unattractive eagerness. Nora had paused, was straddling her bike in front of our house. She was wearing pink ballet slippers and culottes, with a frilly T-shirt. Lace ran in two lines down the front and made cap sleeves over her shoulders. She had what looked like a Swiss army knife cinched around a belt loop, and I thought how like a Swiss army knife she was, all different looks and purposes at the ready. She could open a can with that mouth, for sure.

She looked up, expertly dropping a match as it neared her fingers. She stubbed it out with a pink toe.

"Do you want some tea?" I barked at her, surprising myself with a voice that was not my own, but much worse.

"Juice, if you have some."

She propped her bike against the door of the garage, with a clang. She came back to the door, stood silent in front of me for a whole minute. A newspaper fell from the bike.

"Nora."

She stuck out her hand.

"Neil."

How do you do, how do you do.

I opened the door and she came in. She pushed off her shoes with her toes, grabbing my shoulder when she lost her balance. The kettle was whistling and we took the stairs two at a time. I poured some juice into a red cup and sat it in front of Nora, who was sitting at my dad's seat around the table. We looked at one another. She fit so nicely in the kitchen chair. A straight line of a body. It made the whole table look more sophisticated, and made me take stock of the rest of the room. I looked around as though I'd never seen it before—the knickknacks, bad art, the school photos on the fridge. Did her mom have a photo of her in braces? She was humming and tapping her fingers.

"Do you like to dance?" she asked me. "I can teach you. It's a good thing to know, dancing. In case you're ever invited to a wedding or something."

She smirked at my blank face.

"But, um, not if you don't want." She shrugged.

My loss.

"I taught my brother, though. It's easy."

I didn't know what to say, and so said nothing, which was likely worse. I didn't know how to dance, no, but the prospect of being in dancing proximity to this girl wonder was too much. I opened my mouth and closed it again.

"Um. Where do you live, anyway?" I asked, after a while.

"Neptune."

Nora took my hand in her dry, firm grip and pulled me to the middle of the kitchen. She smelled like peanut butter and smoke, and she hummed softly in a bad soprano. *One two three. One two three.* My palms sweat, staining through her shirt. Just as I was getting the hang of it, she stopped. I kept going, and stepped on her. She laughed.

"Sorry," she said. We separated, and she bit her thumbnail.

"Want to see something?"

"Sure."

I opened the sliding door to the backyard and we stepped out into the morning heat. My parents were putting in a pool and the builders were at the huge empty hole stage: A dirt and air pool. A ladder descended to its airy depths. Nora climbed down first.

The pool was about twelve feet deep, damp, cool. Sound had a quality that made your ears sort of ring, pulling in things that you couldn't hear up above. It was sort of like swimming. Sounds amplified. Private and close. We knelt down around what I had brought her to see. The dampness had rounded its edges—deformed them—but it was still pretty, it was still delicate, like it was holding on just a little longer, changing in tiny ways each morning. Softening, shifting, sighing into something else. A large bug crawled over one of its bridges and we laughed.

It was a little town. I had brought out my dad's chisels, an old spoon, a knife and a margarine container a couple of weeks before, and had been erecting short and tallish buildings, roads, ditches, valleys and hills. The workmen had been occupied with the shallow end of the construction, and when I came out in the evenings, after dinner, in the quiet, the deep-end village was untouched, save for the odd leaf blocking a road. Rain had held off, but I'd been expecting my luck to run out soon.

Nora walked her fingers over one of the structures, and knocked on its door with her middle finger. Sound from above us travelled down, we could hear the neighbours in the house behind. They had a pool—one with water—and now the kids were cannonballing and screaming in the wet and splash, and the sound of them filled the cavernous hole. I felt anxious, on the edge of something. Nora dug her bare toe into the clay and dragged it in a zigzag, away from the back of a little dirt house.

"This is the back way in," she told me. "Good for sneaking."

I cupped my hands over a round building that was losing its shape. I smoothed it out and repositioned the pebbles that bordered its walkway. She took one pebble and with it made a doorknob.

We heard the sliding door open, and we looked up.

"What the hell are you doing in there?"

My brother. We could see him from our vantage point; he was standing there in his jogging pants, scratching his balls and yawning. We stood, careful not to tread on anything. I glanced sideways at Nora. She was looking hard at my brother, the asshole in the jogging pants.

"Oh, what'dya got, someone in there with you?"

He chortled, rudely, and then fixed Nora with a mean look. "Hey... Aren't you our *paper boy*? Jesus."

Nora hit her knees and bum, hard, to knock off the excess dirt. "See you," she mumbled, and climbed up the ladder. My brother laughed. He ignored her as she squeezed past him to get back inside. I stayed where I was.

"Did you drink all the juice, little pervert? Or did your girlfriend?" He shook his head and went inside.

I heard a dull bike bell and then there was only quiet, save for some splashing from the neighbours'. I looked down at the little town, then drew a box around it with my toe, almost losing my balance with the last line.

Daycare

ADA SHIFTED HER DAUGHTER to her right knee. Charlie, four, pumped the train seat beside her with his fist, singing softly. She watched through the window as Toronto faded out; in its place, snowy cherry trees. Soon, tall faded grasses shot up close to the tracks and whipped the glass, blocking out the sun. The train seemed a fast secret, cutting through plant life. Ada wondered how small she would be next to those grasses. They looked to be taller than the train itself.

Her daughter, unnamed for a week due to an indecisiveness that struck Ada like a virus after childbirth, was called Ivy. She was four months old now, and presently she laughed and grabbed at Ada's hair. They were on their way back home. They lived in Niagara Falls, but Ada had never taken the children to the falls. She and Mac had been when they first moved to the town four years ago. They had brought plastic champagne glasses, and had laughed while they toasted with non-alcoholic sparkling wine their new home and Ada's pregnancy. It was nice. But still, there were other places to take the children. Saturdays, to the carousels of Port Dalhousie, the Book Depot in St. Catharines. In Toronto, they looked through storefront windows and walked through the St. Lawrence Market pointing out flowers and pig's ears and fresh fish on ice, while tall, smartly dressed professionals whizzed around them, in suits even on weekends.

Her son and daughter. Charlie twisted in his seat, then stood, staring solemnly at the passenger behind him. Ada brought him down gently with a tug on his T-shirt and handed him half of the cookie she was breaking for Ivy. She wasn't sure when she had started calling them My Son and Daughter. Certainly not when Charlie was first born, small and soft.

Calling him her Son resounded with the voices of older, more matronly women whose children gave their parents trouble. My Son rolled off the tongue. *My Son tells me that it was actually Your Son who was doing the bullying. My Son has got this girlfriend now and you won't believe what she wears.* But she had adapted to this and she did have a son and daughter and had to call them something, eventually, other than 'the baby.'

Ada rubbed Charlie's pale fingers between her own, and pretended to bite one off, before he yanked it irritably to his chest.

"On the other hand, who has time? Some of us work, you know?"

Ada nodded at Mrs. Nicholson while struggling to take off the Nicholson boy's ski jacket. He stared at her neutrally.

"Oh God, Ada, I didn't mean it like that. I just mean real jobs, you know. *This* is a real job. Just that some people think that we can do it all, you know? Jonathan, take that out of your mouth. Here." Mrs. Nicholson put out her hand and Jonathan pushed a wad of wet, blue paper into its palm. Ada reached for another child who had come in with her mother. The girl stuck out her right foot and allowed for its boot to be tugged off and lined up on a puddled plastic mat with the others. Her jacket was hung on one of the twelve coat hooks nailed below the fish and snowflakes and stars which Ada had cut out of differently coloured construction paper. The paper had started to curl and tear.

She glanced at the woman. Mrs. Nicholson was plump, she wore makeup that made her look older than she was, not to mention the fur coat.

"I have to run. Thanks, Ada. I better go before Jonathan sees me and starts bawling."

Mrs. Nicholson squeezed her way past other parents and toddlers, and made her way up the linoleum stairs to the main floor. Ada assembled some of the youngsters in a huddled group on the rug. It was an old rug, one Ada's mother-in-law had brought back from a trip to the Middle East during her travelling years, black and red with white stars that had become grey. In some parts of the room the rug reached the panelled wall and worked its way up. In other sections it gaped over the cold floor.

The children were chatting nonsensically, some shyly touching other children's hair or shoulders, others sucking their thumbs and surveying the room. Charlie was bored and annoyed. He pushed himself along the rug, backwards, on his bum. Ada knew he didn't like having all the other children here, never had, and now that he was as old as the others he was bossy and territorial. Ivy was asleep upstairs in her room, and Ada briefly thought of her, half wishing that she were up there as well, in the dry and quiet room that smelled of talcum, everything soft and clean, glassy-eyed stuffed toys staring from the bookcase.

"Charlie, will you come join us, please?" said Ada.

"No," said Charlie, shuffling sulkily toward her.

Ada opened a large and worn book and began reading.

Ada and Mac had bought their house with the intention of doing a lot of renovations. New floors, new tiles, newness that said, It's Ours. *Ours.* Ada had never done any kind of fixing up, and neither, it turned out, had Mac. And so the red brick two-storey spoke more of the people who used to own the house; the loud young parents who had laughed with Ada and Mac like old and awkward friends, outdoing each other in humour and stories and volume. Ada had tried to remove the personal stain, but the house held strong, long scratches left by a golden lab, holes made by nails from which crucifixes had hung to bless doorways and linen closets, cold linoleum with black scuffs made by an eleven-year-old's tap shoes. But it was quaint country, just as they'd wanted. It was tall and proud with a nice face and a large lot. The street was quiet and had a number of lovely old homes that housed the kind and the chatty, the handy and the nosey. Ada had tried to secure for herself a distance from the neighbours, relying on her city-self, had waved to them above her snow shovel, or from her car, without invitation or snobbery. But they had all peered in anyway. The secret tombs of other people's lives were shut behind lock, key and a stiff smile. But they'd all been to Ada's. They had inhaled her house's odour, that great private identifier, with their first step. They had stolen peeks at family photos and caught sight of delivered flowers. They couldn't help seeing bills and books on the table, clothes tossed over the radiator. They heard Mac looking for his briefcase, or popping toast out of the toaster. They marched their children past the living room and down to the basement, which between themselves seemed a little damp for children.

Ada was slim and young, and aloof because she could be. She had a quiet laugh, small feet, a pianist's fingers and a fast metabolism, which permitted hamburgers and cake. She had an even look, unmoved by leaps of expression. She blinked instead of nodding, nodded instead of saying, *Uh huh, right, I know exactly what you mean*. She provoked love and resentment despite her attempts to prevent either.

She used to be a teller at a bank in Toronto. She had customers who brought her biscotti at Christmas, but was happy to be simply the hands that changed money. She had a name tag with a plastic sticker and a younger man with a crush on her who worked two wickets down. When she'd leave at the end of the day, she'd take her Tupperware container with the remains of her lunch, and a novel she read on her breaks, stowed in a large leather bag. She'd push through the smudged glass door and walk west to the subway, shoes clicking, looking in windows or entering a store if she saw something that would make her look graceful and daring. Usually black or brown. Sweaters and skirts. Bags. Shoes.

Ada and Mac moved to Niagara Falls because with Mac's work they could live anywhere and what a lark to look at homes in Niagara Falls. What a lark, at first. But then they found the tall red house with the nice face and the fix-up potential, and with the bump growing in Ada's midsection, pushing out her black sweaters, they made a giggling decision followed by non-alcoholic champagne poured above the wonder of the world.

She agreed to look after other women's children sort of as

practice. She was due in three months, and preoccupied, and nervous about her abilities as a mother. She didn't tell the other women that. Ada hadn't wanted to apply herself to new work since their move, and lounged lazily in a large chair, slumped, with a slender leg slung over the side, looking out the windows at the trees. Mac would never think ill of her, expectant first-time mother that she was, and to the contrary, he thought her altruistic for offering her services as a nanny of sorts.

At night Ada and Mac would kneed their fingers in the dark. She would tuck her knees up into him, bend her forehead into his chin. Her eyes stayed open for a long time. She counted herself to sleep: twenty, forty, sixty, eighty, her thumbs twitching, peeling off phantom bills.

It was the end of the day. Ada and the children were once again assembled on the floor and Ada was trying to tell them to remember to bring macaroni the next day. She had their attention, and, smiling, invited them to get their mats out of the trunk. They were to lie down now. Ada would lie down too. She had accumulated a number of yoga mats from a club that had had the right idea in the wrong town, and she kept them in a black antique trunk. Every day the children would line the basement with pink and purple and blue mats, staring at the ceiling boards, breathing and counting, or singing, or talking to themselves.

A loud, disturbing, whirring sound came from upstairs. Some of the children stopped and looked up, their fingers in their mouths. Ada went upstairs quickly, then slowed to stand at the sliding door which faced the backyard. Her neighbour's large butternut tree, which sheltered much of Ada and Mac's yard, its green nuts bouncing off their roof and its leaves providing shade in the sticky summer, was coming apart in large pieces, the wood creaking and cracking and falling. A man with a chainsaw was up in the tree. A huge branch came away and fell on Ada's side of the fence. She opened the door and walked out onto the cold deck. The man saw her and started to yell something over the noise. She couldn't understand. He turned it off.

"It was overdue," he shouted. "It wasn't doing anyone any

good. It's dead, y'see? Almost came down in the last storm."

Most of the tree had been cut, and now Ada had an unobstructed view of the old cemetery a block over. She hugged herself. The chainsaw was turned back on, and Ada went inside the house.

The children were still flat on their mats. Some sang quietly or stared. They lay there and hummed and rubbed their feet together, and Ada knew they were counting the holes in the ceiling, as high as they could count. She sat on the top of the trunk and patted down her long pocketed sweater. The chainsaw had stopped again. She found what she was looking for and withdrew a cigarette from the pack. She lit it and inhaled, pulling a small ashtray out of another pocket and placing it on the floor between her feet. Her legs were open and she rested her elbows on her thighs. She looked at the prostrate youngsters and had the urge to talk to them. She knew exactly what she wanted to tell them. She flicked an ash in the tray and opened her mouth.

Later, when the sun had gone down, Ada ventured outside. A strong wind blew. She walked over to the large branch that had landed on her side of the fence, and knelt down. It didn't look dead to her. But she wasn't a great judge of this sort of thing. Perhaps she could use the branch, make a wreath or something. She heard a door close inside the house. Mac was home. She knew he was putting down his briefcase, taking off his overcoat, calling out to her. She snapped a small twig, and the sound was louder than she'd expected.

Butterfly Net

IT WAS ONE OF MY LAST SUMMERS at home, but I didn't know it yet. I was bored and bitter, moods that should have tipped me off, but didn't. The heat was heavy and it rippled through the house, even after dark. Each night, as the front door shut silently behind me, everyone sleeping and sweating and snoring inside, I could hear other teenagers, blocks away, heading out also, or coming home. Sometimes I would put the car in neutral and try to roll out of the driveway, as though I were sneaking away rather than just heading off to my next shift. Night shift appealed to my melancholy mind, justified a moodiness which extended into my voice and actions, my posture and expressions. My car smelled of coffee and cigarettes. At work I would read. Kingsley Amis. Timothy Findley. Comic books. I listened to surf rock and pretended I lived elsewhere, somewhere where I did not work at the Crisco factory, watching security cameras for eight hours.

My family members seemed like cut-outs to me. They were familiar, but so plain, two-dimensional. My dad in particular, soft and simple, was only what remained of the emperor of my childhood. My father wasn't a mean man. He wasn't rough, or sarcastic, or rude. He didn't have cigarette breath, didn't get in fights, didn't let his tie hang loose with a glass of whisky in his hands when he got home from work. He wasn't an insurance salesman who was about to go mad and wipe out his whole family. He didn't work on an assembly line. He didn't lay brick. He didn't even have an old, beat up recliner that was his pride and joy, much to the frustration of our mother. In fact, he was happy to sit on a brand new couch when he watched TV—as good as anywhere. My father worked at the phone company, in a management position that paid pretty well, with benefits for thirty-two years. He had recently retired. He ate toast and dipped it in his tea. He smiled politely when we gave him gifts that he probably didn't like. He fiddled under the hood of the car and listened to the Righteous Brothers.

"Goddamned butterflies." He put on the windshield wipers. My mother sat beside him, my sister and I were in the back. His hair was mashed up against the headrest. We'd been at the cottage all week, in the haze and mosquitoes, and dirt, not sand, had settled in our shoes, our hair, the folds of our arms. We smelled of campfire and mildew.

It was butterfly season.

"I wish they would just fly over the car. Can't they just fly over the car?"

Butterflies flew at the car, hit the window and bounced off. Smudge. Swear. Repeat. I had been sleeping, and soon lifted out of my stupor to recognize the gas station and pizza place near our house. My father pulled into the driveway, and much stretching and gathering of crosswords and tapes ensued, the turning of the key. I watched my father's back as he disappeared into the house.

My father. I could beat him in basketball. Had heard all of his stories. I was suspicious of him all of a sudden. I doubted him. His warmth chilled me. I started to frown at him.

"How are you, Champ?"

"Fine."

"How's the night shift? Getting enough sleep?"

"Yeah."

"Would you rather take my car? I can look at yours, make sure it's safe."

"No, thanks. It's fine."

One early morning not long after the trip to the cottage, I was coming home from work, driving down our street as the sun made its way over the houses, when I saw my father pulling out of the driveway. I could see a bit of his profile as he put his arm around the passenger seat and backed out, with caution, just as he had shown me to do when he taught me to drive. He fixed his hair in the rear-view mirror, readjusted the mirror, drove away. I didn't pull into the driveway, I kept driving, following my father. I followed him from a distance as he drove through the neighbourhood, onto the main street. I followed him around corners, and paused while a woman and her three children crossed in a lopsided line past the stop sign in front of him. He pulled into the grocery store. I parked, too, and walked in after him. I stood inside the doors, watched him round the meat section. I feigned interest in the adjacent aisles, watched him choose ground beef for the barbeque. He smiled and raised a hand in greeting to the butcher. Turned the package over in his hands and tossed it into his cart. A display of children's birthday candles and balloons caught his eye. I saw him smile faintly. He hesitated, threw some candles in the cart as well. I went back to the car and waited. I watched him return to his car, plastic bags digging into his palms. I followed him to the movie store. I followed him to the liquor store.

I followed him all summer.

I didn't have a good reason. I don't know why I wanted to come to know my father as he was, in secret, or rather, in public, that other form of secrecy. My suspicion of him gave way to overactive imagination. He was having an affair. He had other children. I waited. He really was no different. No different than the man who knocked on the bathroom door when I was too long in the shower, or the man who pushed his plate back when he was done eating. He wasn't leading another life apart from the one he led with my mother at home, with her local paper and cup of tea. He left the house and did all the things he said he was going to do.

"I'm going to the corner store for some butter," he'd call. Then he'd buy butter. I'd follow him. The door would ring when we both entered, me a few minutes behind him. I chose carefully where I hid. Not by the magazines, in case he was a pervert and was going to peruse *Hustler* or something. Not by the flowers—maybe he would buy some for his girlfriend. I'd wait by the maxi pads and diapers. He bought butter and paid with exact change.

"Wait—I have 15 cents."

"Thank you. Have a great day, sir."

"You too, now. Almost done your shift?"

"Yes, sir."

"Great. Don't get into too much trouble, now." A smile. The bell ringing him out. Suspicious eyes following me and my hurried, empty-handed exit.

I started to find him likeable. He wasn't dramatic or complicated, but something about that ginger-haired man and the self-conscious smile that he had only for strangers was endearing in a way that his blatant affections were no longer. I felt sorry for him. I was sleepy and teenaged, and doggedly following my fifty-two-year-old father around a bored and witless town. I'd slip into the house after him, mumble hellos and fall into my bed ready for dreams of the weird, daytime kind. It was a hot August. I'd tumble to sleep as the sun made its way into the sky and I could hear in the background the din of pots and pans and parental discourse.

One Sunday he asked me to help in the garden. A large root bulb from a dead cedar needed digging out, and he couldn't do it alone. I stomped on the heel of the shovel, digging into the hard, clay soil around the bulb. My shirt was soaked with sweat, and I cursed the sun and my cigarette habit. My sister, who had been at the other side of the garden picking tomatoes, breezed past me and tossed a rotten one at my feet on her way inside. Our backyard was dense with green bushes and trees and vegetables, grown so that we could hardly see the backyards around us. My dad, in front of me, wielded his own shovel with ease, and I told myself that he was standing in the shade even though he was squinting in the light. He had cut the cedar down to waist height, its pale needles and dry branches forming a ring around the base.

"I planted this thing fifteen years ago. So we could have privacy." He chuckled. "They were pretty expensive back then, and someone told me not to get more than one 'cause if one gets a disease, the others can catch it, and then they'll all die like big green dominos." He wiped his brow. "I just got this one."

I looked at the body of the tree and grasped it, then tried

shaking it to see if we'd made any progress. It moved almost imperceptibly, like a loose tooth.

"Is that why this one died? Disease?"

"I guess. Or old age, neglect, too much sun, loneliness. Who knows. I probably didn't plant it in the best spot. Was thinking impulsively, which is the worst trait in a gardener."

He leaned back on the shovel and the bulb started to rock slightly. I did the same. My shovel strained in my hands. He dug around the sides, digging a trench and revealing the scraggy root bulb with its thick fingers that reached down and out. I coughed, and it turned into a small fit. He watched me, a small smile on his face.

"So! They treating you well at the job?" I gasped and nodded my head, and began digging again. "Good." I could tell there was more. I felt the tip of the spade dig into the meat of the roots, but not deep enough. "Have you thought any more about schools? Which ones? For what?" My parents had always been rather hands-off when it came to school, and I'd always done well. Up until now the topic of university had been glazed over, which I found slightly unsettling, given the involvement of my friends' parents in their futures. I looked up at him.

"Actually, I'm not really sure what I want to do. Or why." I could tell my frankness took him slightly off guard, as it did me.

"Oh. Yes, well, it's a big decision." He picked dirt out of his fingernails, and shook his head.

"Lemme take that back. No, you know, that's true, it is a big decision, but it's not the end or anything. You can restart or change your mind all sorts of times. That's something no one ever tells you. That no one's going to hold you to your decisions like it's some kind of contract."

This was news to me.

"I'm sure it'll come to me, what I want to do, but, I dunno. I just sort of like to read. Like, stories. What am I supposed to do with that?"

"Well, I wouldn't recommend engineering."

I laughed at this.

"Hey, I studied Philosophy. Your granddad asked me when I was going to get a job at the Philosophy factory to support my family. That was before I married his daughter and he had to stop acting like an ass to me."

With a last push on the end of his shovel, the bulb shifted heavily. I repositioned mine and tried to mimic him. I stepped hard on the spade and leaned down and back on the wooden handle. With a crack, it snapped in my hands, sending me stumbling, cutting my hand through my work glove. He dropped his shovel and came to my side, offering his hand to better see mine. He took off the glove, we watched the blood come to the surface of my palm. He looked back at the bulb, which had keeled over, and said, "Let's call it a day. Thanks, Son. That's a real help. We'll get that fixed up," he said, gesturing to my hand. I followed him inside.

Sometime around the end of August, my father exited the IGA around nine in the morning. He was pushing a cart with a bum wheel. He kept checking the wheel to see which way it was facing. I was parked across the street. He pushed through the empty parking lot as a car pulled in, a beat-up station wagon with wood panelling. I couldn't see what was happening, but had a bad feeling about it. I had a feeling of my father being hassled. The passengers in the station wagon looked to be teenagers, one of them appeared to have a plastic windmill, which he was poking out the window. I leaned over my steering wheel to get a better angle, and saw my father fall to the ground, his cart tipping over. I left my car running and dodged across the road.

Someone from the car had opened the door, banging the tipped-over cart, and was getting out of the car. He looked like a regular guy, but I knew better, and tried to shove him back into his seat. He held onto the door and regained his balance.

"What the—"

He took a swipe at me, catching me on the chin slightly as I ducked backward and tripped over my father's prone body. There was a confused moment when everyone was speaking at once, and my father seemed to be apologizing to his aggressors, but I assumed he meant to direct this to me. I rubbed my chin and offered my hand to help my father up. He slapped it away and got up on his own. The teenagers eventually drove off.

"I think we'd better get you a day job," he said. I stared. "Those guys weren't going to hurt me, they were asking for directions. I tripped because of this damn cart. What did you think they were going to do, rob me for my ice cream? They had a kid in the backseat, you know."

He touched his finger to his lip and looked at it. "You gave me a bloody lip. And you should stop following me, for godsakes. And stop leaving your car running. Someone's looking to steal it."

I turned around and saw that he was right. Two thin underagers were looking in the car windows. I ran across the road.

I stopped following my father. He didn't tell my mother or sister, which I thought was very charitable. I did get a day job, at the library, which actually permitted less reading than the security guard job. I stacked books, and let the sun come in the window on my eyes. Children ran around me, choosing creased books about animals and dragons and giants. I met a girl. A girlfriend. My father would call her 'your girl' or 'his girl' like we were in *American Graffiti*. I was happy. I had left my wakeful nights behind, left my ashes in the backseat.

The following summer, my father and I drove up to the cottage together in my car. My sister and mother had gone ahead, because I had to work and my father made an excuse to stay and keep me company on the drive up. We had the windows open and we were quiet for the most part. The breeze blew between us and ruffled the pages of maps and books. We could smell the lake long before we could see it.

"We should go fishing. Did you remember your pole?"

"I left it up there last time."

"Perfect."

Later that week, my sister and I were out together in the canoe. We'd actually become quite good. Our arms mirrored each other, the paddles sliced quietly through the water. There was so little noise. And then our mother was hollering, waving, calling down the slope from the cottage to the water's edge. We laughed nervously because she seemed so silly, waving and yelling, tripping through the sand in her strappy sandals. There was something. Suddenly we knew there was something. It felt like forever, paddling back to shore.

We had a lovely service, everyone said so. I used to think that was a stupid thing to say. But it was true. I met cousins and friends whom I'd never met before. Everyone told me I looked just like him. It was nice, sort of. We put up pictures of him in his fishing gear and laid his hat with the flies on it on the coffin. I cried. I cried like nobody's business and I didn't care what that looked like. I drove around listening to sad music. The Righteous Brothers. I couldn't roll up the windows, especially on the passenger side.

I stayed up there all summer. I was planning to move out in the fall, and was in no hurry, all of a sudden, to go home and pack my bags. I breathed in the lake, the dirt, the leaves, like they were lines I had to memorize. One hot afternoon, I walked around the back of the cottage, kicking pebbles. It was butterfly season. They seemed to follow me around. I was afraid to touch them because I'd heard that if you touch them they die. I looked at the dead ones on the ground near the car. I picked some up. They were so delicate. I thought of pinning them to a board, but couldn't bear it. I lay them in a line on the trunk of the car and got in. I started the car, put it into drive, hit the gas. In the rearview, I could see them stick for a second, then they stirred and the wind picked them up and whirled them around like leaves. I looked ahead as they started to fall.

Acknowledgements

I would like to thank Beth Follett for her insight, her care and her warmth.

Nicole and Kristen and Karen and Donna: thank you for years of eyes and ears.

Mom and Dad and Michael: thank you for your love and support, which seem to know no bounds.

Jay: thank you for it all, for everything.

Eli: thank you for coming. You're the life of our party.

JAY JOHNSTON, 2005

LAURIE PETROU lives in Grimsby, Ontario. She is an assistant professor of digital media and design at the School of Radio and Television Arts at Ryerson University in Toronto. This is her first book.